MY SECRET LIFE IN PARIS

LUCY SALISBURY

T0317992

mischief

Mischief
An imprint of HarperCollins*Publishers*
77–85 Fulham Palace Road,
Hammersmith, London W6 8JB

www.mischiefbooks.com

A Paperback Original 2013

First published in Great Britain in ebook format by
HarperCollins*Publishers* 2012

A catalogue record for this book is
available from the British Library

ISBN-13: 9780007553297

Find out more about HarperCollins and the environment at
www.harpercollins.co.uk/green

CONTENTS

CONTENTS

Chapter One

Paris, the last day of spring, the scent of fresh-baked bread in the air and the strains of *la Marseillaise* faint in the distance. Paris, the Aire de Villabé, a truckstop on the E15, the taste of a long-haul driver's cock in my mouth and the feel of his hand on my bare skin as he fondled my bottom. Ah, romance!

Well, dirty, smutty, shame-filled sex anyway, but I wasn't complaining. After years of reserved, correct behaviour as I climbed the greasy pole of corporate success I'd finally managed to live out one of my favourite fantasies, being made to pay for a lift by sucking the driver's penis. Well, not *made* exactly, because both Claude and Jean-Luc had taken quite a bit of persuading before accepting that the very English blonde they'd offered a lift was really up for it, but once they'd got the idea they'd both been everything I could have hoped for.

Three times Jean-Luc had made me go down on him during the long drive, and now was my fourth, and last, to say thank-you for my lift before going into the city to take up my place as 2IC in the company's French office. I was taking my time, savouring the taste and feel of his cock in my mouth and enjoying the mauling he was giving my bottom, with his hand well in down the back of my panties and one finger teasing the mouth of my cunt. He'd fucked me the night before, with my thighs spread to his thrusts in the little sleeping space at the rear of his cab, but the Aire de Villabé was a little too public for me to strip off, for all that my jeans were already unfastened and my jumper and top up over my boobs.

I was fairly sure I was about to get my mouthful when he did it, suddenly and with no warning at all. He didn't even bother to ask, but merely pulled me off his cock, flipped me over and scrambled around to mount me from behind. I hadn't even had a chance to get my jeans and panties down properly before he was up me, his massive, calloused hands gripping my hips as he pushed his cock in. Fortunately I was soaking wet and took it easily, but as I came up onto my hands and knees to get more comfortable I found myself looking out of the cab window and through another, into the face of the astonished driver.

For one awful moment we were staring eye to eye, no more than a few feet apart, before I put my head down, my face now burning with blushes and painfully aware that he still had a prime view of my upturned white bottom as I got humped from behind. I was sure he could even see Jean-Luc's cock going in and out, but my babbled pleas were ignored and my struggles achieved nothing, my hips held in a grip like a vice. If he even knew then he didn't care, thrusting ever harder into me and grunting like a bull gorilla as I squirmed on his cock, then suddenly whipping it free – not out of sympathy for my embarrassment, but to finish himself off all over my bare bottom, in full view of the other man.

I was left like that, wide-eyed in shock and humiliation, my rear cheeks sticking up like a pair of plum puddings with cream topping running down the sides and his cock rearing up between them as he gave himself a last little rub in my slit, then considerately wiped my bottom down with an oily rag. And that was that, my thank-yous said, my shame and embarrassment brought to a final peak, as wonderful as it was unexpected. I hadn't even explained to Jean-Luc what I liked. He'd just used me, without the slightest thought for my privacy or dignity, an unspeakable thing to do to a woman – and exactly the sort of thing that's always going on in my head when I come.

I didn't know whether to thank him or slap him, but I've always been taught not to make a fuss so I simply adjusted my clothes, tidied up as best I could, retrieved my shoulder bag from the sleeping cubicle, kissed him goodbye and left. The man who'd watched me get my fucking was still staring, and he wasn't the only driver in his cab along the line of maybe thirty lorries, which left me with a long walk of shame, pink-faced with embarrassment and painfully aware that at least a dozen pairs of eyes were fixed on my rear view as I made for the services.

Fortunately there were lots of facilities, allowing me to make myself look more or less normal, if not actually respectable. My intention had been to end up looking like a smart, professional woman fresh off the Eurostar and not a dirty little tramp fresh off a lorry driver's cock, but thanks to Jean-Luc's rough handling I hadn't quite succeeded. I'd repaired my make-up and put my hair up in a bun instead of the long blonde ponytail that had allowed me to pass for a student hitch-hiker, but there was no dealing with the oily handprints on the flesh of my hips and bottom cheeks, and on my jeans. Anybody who gave me more than a cursory inspection was going to realise that I'd been fucked from behind, but I had it all under control.

One of the good things about being turned on by embarrassment is that I can cope with things that would leave many women wanting to curl up into a ball. Another is that I've gained plenty of experience in extricating myself from awkward situations. I plan, and this occasion was no exception, but I still started at the sudden sharp voice from behind me.

'What would do you good, Lucy, is a taste of the whip.'

I'd dropped my lip-gloss and had to squat down and scrabble under the sinks to get it, which put a small, cruel smile on the face of the woman who'd spoken. She had pronounced my name in the French fashion and she looked the part too, quintessentially French and Parisienne – petite, with dark hair cut in a gamine style and wearing skintight black jeans and a cream-coloured roll-neck sweater.

'You made me jump, Adrienne.'

'Not as high as you'd jump to my dog whip. Stick your bottom out.'

'Isn't it a bit public?'

'Stick your bottom out, Lucy.'

I made a face but obeyed, resting my hands on the sinks and pushing out my bottom to accept a single sharp smack across the seat of my jeans. It was given to put me in my place, which was very definitely on the receiving end where Adrienne was concerned. We'd met during my unsuccessful flat-hunting expedition a fortnight before, sharing an encounter in the Bois de Boulogne which had left it very plain that we each had what the other needed. I'd called her as I drove north in Jean-Luc's lorry, but I hadn't expected her to arrive at the Aire de Villabé before me, or to want to assert her dominance on the spot and in the ladies.

A woman came in just as Adrienne's smack landed across my seat: slightly older, very smart in an urbane style, what they call *bon chic bon genre*, and the last person I'd have chosen to watch me get a spanking. Adrienne didn't care, planting a second smack across my bottom as I quickly stood up straight, then marching out of the restroom with me in tow, blushing furiously as I tried to reassert myself with her.

'I'm staying at the Hôtel l'Aigrette in La Défense, if –'

'You're coming with me, for now. We can go to your hotel later.'

'But Adrienne –'

'Be quiet, Lucy. Unless you'd like your bottom smacked again, right here?'

We'd come out to the main area of the services, a huge open space with maybe two hundred people to watch me get it if she carried out her threat. I was fairly sure she didn't mean it, but I didn't want to find out the hard way, so I shut up, while imagining how it would feel to be put across her knee and spanked in front of so many onlookers. She gave a dry chuckle, no doubt fully aware of what was going on in my head.

'You call me out to meet you here, thirty kilometres out of town, and you don't expect to be disciplined? You know how it works, Lucy.'

I did, although I'd expected her to wait until the evening before giving me what I undoubtedly deserved. A man would have done, almost certainly, and probably bought me dinner before coaxing me out of my clothes for punishment and sex, but not Adrienne. She liked to be in charge, in normal life as well as in bed, and that meant doing as I was told. Besides, she was right.

'I'm sorry. Things got rather complicated.'

'So I see. I thought you were coming from Calais?'

'I was, but … but I went to sleep and woke up in Beaune. I had to get another lift.'

'I'm sure you did, instead of taking the train, but then, the SNCF don't take the use of a woman's mouth as payment, do they? Did it work?'

'Yes, both times, both drivers, Claude and Jean-Luc. I can't remember exactly how many times they made me go down on them.'

'I just hope you don't expect me to kiss you. Stay here.'

She turned back and disappeared inside the building, leaving me wondering what was going on. Her little red Renault was parked at the end of a line of cars in front of the services and I went to stand beside it and wait. She came back holding a bottle of water and spoke immediately, her tone firm but also mocking and cruel.

'I said, stay by the doors. Stick out your bottom.'

'But Adrienne, people will see …'

'How many times do I have to give you an order, Lucy? Stick out your bottom.'

I hesitated, but there weren't that many people around and I did want to obey, because the shame of what I'd been ordered to do was just too strong for me to resist.

Anywhere less anonymous and I wouldn't have done it, but, as I turned my back and presented myself for her attention once more, I was reasoning that whatever people might think of a grown woman getting her bottom smacked outside a service station, they wouldn't know that it was me. That only went so far to soothe my feelings as Adrienne's hand landed across my rear cheeks with a sharp double slap. Quite a few people had noticed, and I was left blushing hotter than when I'd walked away from the lorries, but she wasn't finished with me yet.

'Now open your mouth.'

'What –'

My question was abruptly choked off as she thrust something between my lips, a small, hard bar of soap, the sort they'd had in the ladies' restroom. It tasted foul, but there was no mistaking the look on her face and I held it in as she offered the water bottle.

'Take some. Swill it around your mouth. Then get in the car.'

She watched, amused but still full of authority as I took a swallow of water, my expression turning more disgusted by the moment as the soapy taste grew stronger. Yet I knew better than to spit it out and did as I was told, holding my mouthful as I climbed into the passenger seat of the Renault. Adrienne got in beside me and chuckled as she started the car, which was hardly surprising: my cheeks were popping and my eyes beginning to water.

I tried to say something, but soap bubbles immediately started to issue from between my lips, leaving me feeling very sorry for myself indeed and painfully turned on as Adrienne rejoined the motorway, talking as she drove.

'You should see yourself, Lucy. You do look funny, but then, that was my favourite thing about you from the start, the faces you pull when you are punished. I know you love it, but you always look so cross and so stupid at the same time, like you hate to be punished but you can't stop yourself from taking it because you know what it does to you. This is good, because you deserve this, Lucy, for making me come out here, and for being such a slut. I mean, imagine it, allowing lorry drivers to make you suck them off in return for a lift, and more too, I'll bet. Did you let them fuck you, Lucy?'

I nodded, deeply ashamed of myself for what I'd done, her every word pushing my feelings higher. Despite my best efforts to keep my mouth shut the soap bubbles had begun to dribble down my face and were hanging from my chin in a little frothy beard. Adrienne gave a tut of contempt at my confession and carried on.

'I thought as much. You deserve the soap, Lucy, and you deserve what you're going to get back at my apartment.'

She gave me a knowing look as she finished, then turned her attention back to the road. We'd played together twice, and both times she'd whipped me, her favourite sport and probably what she'd had in mind, but that was quite enough. The little plaited leather dog whip she favoured carried an agonising sting, and she had made me take it kneeling with my bare bottom pushed out in a way that left everything on show but carried none of the intimacy of an old-fashioned over-the-knee spanking.

The traffic was getting heavy and Adrienne stopped talking, leaving me to chew on the bar of soap in my mouth and reflect on the situation I'd got myself into. I did like her, and the way she handled me, and I badly needed safe friends in Paris, but she seemed determined to take full advantage of my sexuality, stripping me of every last shred of dignity. Half an hour we'd been together and already I'd had my bottom smacked in public and my mouth washed out with soap, but all I could do was submit and await my chance to teach her how I like to be dealt with.

She lived in the 16th arrondissement, in a small but select attic apartment off the Avenue Mozart, and exactly the sort of place I had my eye on for my own accommodation once I'd settled into my new job. It was more than an hour's drive from the Aire de Villabé, but my mumbled requests to spit the soap out were met with refusal and the promise of additional punishment. By the time we arrived I was beginning to feel sick, my mouth was full of bubbles, and I'd had to puff my cheeks out to stop myself swallowing what was left of the bar.

Adrienne grinned at my discomfort as I climbed from the car, making queer gulping noises and pointing at my mouth as I struggled to communicate my needs without committing open disobedience. She shook her head.

'Not until we're upstairs, little one, and then only because I don't want mess on my carpet.'

I managed a nod, trying to seem genuinely thankful but wondering what would happen if I turned the tables on her and put her over my knee in the street. She was tiny, lightly built, not particularly strong either, while I not only stood nearly a foot taller but had spent most of the spring at an outdoor training camp, making my muscles lean and hard. It would have been the work of a moment to sit down on the bonnet of the Renault, haul her across my lap, get her out of her jeans and the no doubt fancy panties beneath and spank her until she howled.

Unfortunately I believe in consent and she had made it plain from the first that she only gave, never received. That didn't stop me thinking about it as I was dragged upstairs by my ear and pushed in at the door of her flat, where I ran for the bathroom to spend five minutes gagging and spluttering over the sink while she stood watching from the doorway. Even when I'd rinsed my mouth a dozen times I could still taste the soap, and my eyes were watering so badly it looked as if I'd been in tears for hours. She merely nodded as I turned to her for inspection.

'There, and I trust you have learned your lesson? You go with men when I say you go with men. Is that understood?'

I wasn't sure if she meant it or if it was part of the game we were playing, but I didn't want to break the moment so I bowed my head as I answered her.

'Yes, M'selle Adrienne.'

'Good. Now turn around and put your hands behind your back, with your wrists crossed.'

I obeyed, peering back over my shoulder as I offered her my wrists. She was going to tie me, that much was obvious, and it was sure to be to keep me still for whatever punishment was coming, very possibly in some awkward, embarrassing and painful position. Sure enough, she'd no sooner lashed my wrists together then she pulled me, walking backwards, into her living room. I'd been there before, when I was made to kneel on the sofa with my jeans and panties down behind and my top up over my boobs while I was whipped, but this time she threw the tail of the rope over a beam and hauled my arms up behind my back.

'I love this flat,' she said as she did so. 'It could have been designed for dealing with little tarts like you, Lucy. Open your legs, and pull your back in so that sweet little bottom of yours makes a nice shape. You are a woman, Lucy, and should always try to be elegant and poised, even while you're being beaten. Now then, let's have your trousers down, shall we?'

She'd tied the end of the rope to a fitting on the wall and now she put her hands around my waist, pulled open the button of my jeans and unzipped me before tugging them down. My panties followed and I was bare, my bottom fully exposed, not just my cheeks but the rear view of my cunt, and even my anus was on show. I was left like that, shaking badly, the pain already building in my shoulders, as she went into the bedroom to fetch the vicious little dog whip she'd used on me before. She came back and used the whip handle to lift my chin.

'I see you're still dirty from your fucking?'

'I couldn't get the oil off. His ... his hands were dirty, the second lorry driver, Jean-Luc. He took me from behind, holding me by my hips. The man in the next cab saw ... saw me getting fucked.'

'I don't wish to know the details of your sordid encounters, Lucy, just how many times you made the two men come?'

'I ... I don't know. Six? Eight?'

'We'll call it eight, in your mouth, and you let both of them fuck you?'

'Yes, but I was counting that.'

'I wasn't. You get one stroke for each time you let them come in your mouth and two strokes for each time you let them in up your dirty little cunt, got it? That makes twelve.'

'Yes, M'selle Adrienne.'

'Good. I'm glad we understand each other, and in future, if you so much as look at a man without my permission, you get the same treatment. Now then, let's have your pretty little breasts bare, always a good thing for a punished girl.'

'Yes, M'selle Adrienne.'

As she spoke she'd pulled up my top and jumper, leaving my breasts exposed and quivering. My nipples were stiff, and when she noticed she gave another little chuckle, amused and full of contempt for my helpless excitement. She made a loop in the whip and stroked the leather over my skin, tracing the shape of my dangling breasts and teasing my nipples.

'How pathetic you are, Lucy, letting yourself get strung up with your little round bottom all bare and your top pulled up for a whipping – for a whipping, Lucy, like some disobedient slave girl or a reluctant whore way back when. Well, that's what you want, and that's what you're going to get.'

She lashed out with the dog whip, catching me full across my cheeks to lay a line of fire onto my flesh and set me gasping for breath and treading up and down. It hurt like anything, and if I'd been free I'd have tried to stop it, or at least shield my poor burning bottom, but there was nothing I could do. Tied and helpless, I was hers to use as she pleased until she chose to release me, and that meant the full twelve whip strokes, delivered one by one across my naked bottom and hips until I was dancing and jerking on the end of the rope, my hair flying in every direction and my tits jiggling as much as my bottom cheeks.

Adrienne never once spoke, but delivered my whipping with cool detachment, just as if she had been my owner or mistress and I nothing more than a slave girl or a prostitute being given a mechanical, emotionless punishment. I knew it was a lie, and just how excited she was becoming beneath her cool exterior, but even as the twelfth stroke cracked down across my squirming bottom she held her poise. Then she tilted my chin up with the whip handle once more.

'There we are, Lucy, all done, although I have to say that you weren't very dignified about it, wriggling around and squealing like that. Do you know what you remind me of? A piglet, that's what. In fact, I think I shall call you Cochonette in future, at least until you learn to show a little restraint during punishment.'

I didn't answer, looking up at her through the now bedraggled curtain of my hair. My skin was slick with sweat, my bottom a mess of burning welts, my thighs slippery with the juice from my sex, and the humiliating nickname felt exactly right, rather kind even, as if I were a pet, to be named as she pleased, treated when I was good and punished when I was naughty. I nodded my acceptance, but she wasn't content, pushing my chin up a little higher and looking down into my face as she addressed me again.

'What is your new name, Lucy?'

'Cochonette, M'selle Adrienne.'

'Good. I think we are beginning to understand one another. I'm going to enjoy owning you, Lucy, my darling. Now, to judge by the smell of you, you want to come, and so do I.'

I'd expected her to be cruel, perhaps leaving my hands tied behind my back as I was put on my knees to lick her to ecstasy, but she quickly unfastened the knot at my wrists and I felt pathetically grateful as I slumped down to the carpet. My shoulders ached and my welts stung badly, but she was right: more than anything else I needed to come. I stripped off my clothes in seconds and crawled nude across the floor to her. As I buried my face between her thighs to lick her cunt, my fingers were already busy with my own.

Chapter Two

I hadn't bargained for the intensity of Adrienne's feelings for me, nor the way she'd simply taken charge, but over the following couple of weeks I had no time to sort things out with her. She wasn't the first woman who had treated me like that, and not only do I really rather like it, I find it much easier to just go with the flow, especially when I need to exert strong control over other parts of my life. In this case it was work.

In the short time between my appointment and taking up the position, the French had decided to elect a socialist president, with predictable results. Most of the staff had been transferred, either to London or New York, leaving only a handful of key operators. Juniors aside, these were either too old and set in their ways to want to leave, or simply too French. My boss, M. Montesquieu, fell into both categories.

He would roll up at the office in the late morning, make a few kindly but condescending remarks to people, myself included, then disappear into his office, to emerge shortly after noon and roll out again and off to one or another of his favourite restaurants. Occasionally he would come back in the late afternoon, after taking on board at least one bottle of wine, make a few more remarks, some of them close to actionable, then doze off in the enormous black leather chair behind his office desk. To all intents and purposes, that left me in charge, which meant imposing my will on people who resented me for being younger than they were and in charge, for being English or for being a woman – in some cases for all three.

I had to be pin-sharp all day, every day, so that by leaving time it was sheer bliss simply to give in to Adrienne's will. She wasn't even a difficult mistress, because, although she liked to be firmly in control, she believed in punishing me only when I misbehaved. As she was divorced, and in receipt of an ample monthly income from her ex-husband, she had time on her hands. I didn't have to shop or cook, and I was always welcome at her apartment, which was only a couple of doors down from mine in the Rue de la Cure.

For the first week I ate with her every evening and went to bed with her afterwards, only returning to my own flat when I had satisfied both her and myself. It was even possible to get back along the rooftops, as long as I left the window open on the landing. The flat lead roof above her apartment was good for sunbathing, if not perfect, because it was overlooked by several taller apartment buildings, although none of them particularly close. Now she had invited me to join her at the weekend, and I was wondering if she'd make me go topless or even nude, but by the time I left work on the Friday I was in need of something rather more immediate, and preferably both soothing and slightly painful.

The difficulty was M. Montesquieu. It would be wrong to say I found him attractive, at least in the conventional sense, as he was much too old for me, but he was a great bear of a man, which I like, and had a wholly inappropriate and old-fashioned attitude to women, which I don't, but if it's done a certain way I can't stop it getting to me. If he'd been rude, or openly suggestive, I'd have been able to cope, putting him in his place with a few carefully chosen remarks and if necessary threatening to report him to head office. Unfortunately he was invariably polite, but still managed to make me feel very feminine and very vulnerable, in such a way that I couldn't help but imagine what it would be like for him to spank me. Not that I had any reason to think he'd want to do it, or even that he might find the idea appealing, but it's my thing and I couldn't resist thinking about it, with all sorts of peculiar fantasies running through my head as I walked back from the Metro.

First and foremost was the idea of him suddenly deciding

that I was getting too big for my boots and that the best way to cut me down to size would be a spanking in front of the rest of the staff. I'd be made to circulate a memo inviting everybody to watch, perhaps in his office, or on the main floor so that absolutely everybody got to see, including any clients who happened to be about, perhaps a few couriers, repair men, anybody. Inevitably it would be on my bare bottom, to really humiliate me, with my suit skirt rolled up from the start. My panties would be pulled down, but not immediately, only after a few swats, to let me think I might be allowed to keep that last, vital piece of dignity before having my cunt and anus put on show to all the men and women I spent my days ordering around.

I meant to tell Adrienne and beg her to punish me for my dirty and disloyal thoughts, preferably by dealing with me in exactly the same way as I'd been dealt with in my fantasy, minus the large and embarrassing audience. Unfortunately she wasn't there and I was left outside her door, clutching in one hand the bottle of Fleurie I'd picked up at Nicolas and in the other the flowers I'd bought for her. I looked and felt like an abandoned date. She'd said she would be there, and had probably only gone out to the shops, but I'd expected to be across her knee within a couple of minutes of my arrival and my frustration was in danger of boiling over. I tried to call her but there was no response, and with that I decided to take matters into my own hands.

Feeling thoroughly ashamed of myself but all the more excited for that, I went back to my flat, swallowed a glass of the Beaujolais and crawled onto my bed, still on all fours and with my eyes closed as I began to fantasise. In my imagination I was back at the office, my face hot with indignant blushes as M. Montesquieu informed me that I would benefit from ten minutes across his knee with the rest of the staff watching as I was given a spanking. He'd tell me off, calling me a little madam and a spoilt brat, then send me off to distribute the memo, not by email but by hand, with everybody whispering together and smirking over my fall from grace as the message went around.

I needed my bottom smacked, whether it was by M. Montesquieu, Adrienne, the spotty boy who'd served me in Nicolas or myself, which was the only practical choice. Reaching back, I took hold of the hem of my skirt and rolled it slowly up my thighs, imagining how it would feel to have to do it with everybody in the office watching. I was in a slip, but that came up too, and the tail of my blouse, to leave first the tops of my stockings showing, then my panties, taut across my cheeks and distinctly moist where the gusset hugged my cunt.

The shame of having to spank myself was so strong I was sobbing even as I planted the first, firm pat across the seat of my panties, but nothing to what it would have been if it had been M. Montesquieu's huge, fleshy paw.

21

I wondered if I'd have gone meekly or made a fight of
it, kicking and writhing so that I had to be held down
across his lap by force, begging to be let off and promising to be a good girl even as my panties were exposed
behind. He'd take no notice, keeping me firmly in place
as he planted swat after swat across my jiggling cheeks,
just to the point when I'd resigned myself to my fate,
grateful that at least I still had my knickers up, before
telling me they were coming down.

My bottom was already warm and my cunt desperate
for the touch of my fingers, but I forced myself to hold
back until I could concentrate on the most shameful
moment of all, having my already well smacked bottom
stripped bare in front of the watching staff. I took hold
of my panties, imagining that it was not my hand but
M. Montesquieu's, and drew them slowly down. As I did
so, I thought about the awful sense of consternation in
my head as I was laid bare, my bottom exposed despite
my crazy, pathetic struggles to keep myself covered, my
threats, my curses, my appeals to his sense of decency,
all ignored, and as I slowly put myself on show I began
to babble.

'No, please, Monsieur Montesquieu, not my panties,
not that ... at least leave me that. I don't want to be
spanked bare. I don't deserve to be spanked bare, you
pig, you great brute! No, please, they'll see my –'

'Cunt?'

Adrienne had spoken from directly behind me, much as she had at the Aire de Villabé and with even more startling effect, but as I made to turn over she reached out to place a restraining hand in the small of my back.

'Oh, no, you don't, Lucy, you stay like that and think about what you were doing while I tell you off.'

I obeyed, my head thick with chagrin for the position I was being made to hold, my bottom stuck up in the air and my panties rolled down to the tops of my stockings. But I was puzzled too. Adrienne was quick to explain.

'I let myself in with the key I had cut the other day, when you lent me yours so that I could air your flat properly. Although as a general rule girls who masturbate ought to make sure they put the latch on first, and close the shutters. Didn't I tell you about old Commandant Arnauld? He has an apartment at the back, with a roof garden. He likes to watch me sunbathing, and I imagine he can see into your window quite well.'

'My modesty curtains are closed, but thank you anyway.'

'Would you thank me if I opened them, right now?'

'Adrienne, no!'

'Why not? He's a war hero. You should be more generous, and besides, from what I heard, you were fantasising about being spanked by your boss, with your knickers pulled down. That would be the Monsieur Montesquieu you were telling me about, I suppose. How old is he?'

23

'That … that's not the same thing at all, Adrienne! I was only thinking about it. Now please can I roll over? This is embarrassing!'

'Stay as you are, it's supposed to be embarrassing. But don't worry, I'll spare your blushes and leave the curtains closed, if only because old Arnauld isn't the only neighbour at the back and I don't want any complaints, especially as I am going to punish you.'

I didn't answer, confused, deeply embarrassed and more ashamed of myself than ever, but desperately in need of what she was planning for me. She'd stepped away from the bed as she spoke, presumably to find something to beat me with. I'd have far preferred to be dealt with across her knee and by hand, but I'd not yet had a chance to teach her the virtues of English corporal punishment.

But at least some of them seemed to be popular in France too. After a moment's thought she picked up the fluffy white bath towel I'd put out over the back of a chair. Memories flooded in, of having my bottom flicked as, naked and dripping, I ran a gauntlet of laughing girls, the wet ends of the towels cracking against my bare flesh, with Juliette Fisher at the far end to catch me and hold me while the others took turns to enjoy a little target practice. Unfortunately Adrienne didn't seem to be very good at it, for she folded the towel along its length instead of twisting it from corner to corner, and it was still dry.

'You have to wet it first, Adrienne, or at least the tip, then you hold it up and spin it to make it work like a whip.'

'Whatever are you talking about?'

'How to use the towel to whip me.'

'I said I was going to punish you, Lucy, not whip you. My whip is in my apartment, for one thing, and there's not a great deal of point in spanking you, is there? You like it too much.'

'Oh ... please, Adrienne? It still hurts, and you can use my hairbrush if you like, or I'll teach you how to use a wet towel.'

'You're a disgrace, Lucy. Now kneel up on the bed. That's right, knees apart, and keep your skirt up.'

I obeyed, puzzled, as she cocked one leg up on the bed beside me in order to thread the towel between my thighs and pull it up, covering my back and front with the thick, soft material. As she began to tie the corners together at my hips I realised what she was doing.

'Adrienne! No, you can't put me in nappies, no ...'

'I rather think I just have, and why not? It suits you to be made a big baby, especially with your nappy on under your business suit.'

My answer was a sulky, choking sob, because that was all I could manage for the thought of what she was doing to me, and she was right. It did suit me, because it was hard to imagine anything more shameful than a fully grown woman being made to wear a nappy, unless perhaps it was wearing a nappy underneath a smart business suit. I let her do it though, my head full of consternation as she tied the corners of the towel at my hips to leave my bottom and belly encased in thick white towelling with a knot sticking out at either side. She then stood back.

'Very pretty. Now pull your knickers up over the towelling.'

I obeyed, looking daggers at her as I wriggled my panties back up over my nappy-clad bottom until they were stretched taut, the towelling bulging out from the leg-holes and the twin knots hanging out at my hips. Adrienne gave her light, cruel chuckle.

'Go and look at yourself in the mirror, Lucy.'

My wardrobe door was a full-length mirror, and I only had to shuffle a little way up the bed to see my reflection: my upper body fully dressed, as neat and correct as could possibly have been asked, in appalling contrast to the huge, fluffy nappy bulging my expensive black lace panties. I looked both ridiculous and grossly indecent, a girl done up as a painfully humiliating punishment or for perverted sex, maybe both. Adrienne gave me a moment to reflect on the state I was in, then spoke again.

'I thought that might get to you, Lucy. Now pull your skirt down.'

I tried, but it wouldn't go, leaving a good deal of my nappy showing both back and front, while I had to pull the knots up over the waistband on either side. By then Adrienne was laughing openly, and I had to admit that if it had been another girl in nappies rather than me I'd have done the same. As it was I was left choking with shame and unable to pull my gaze away from the mirror as Adrienne continued to give her instructions.

'That's right, very good, Lucy. Now turn your back to me and stick your bottom out. Superb, truly comic! Now to the mirror ... yes, that's right, darling, what a sight you are! Now face me and pull up the front of your skirt. Yes, just like that, and hold still, with that priceless expression on your face.'

She'd pulled out her phone and I realised she was going to take a picture, at which I rebelled.

'No, Adrienne, seriously, no pictures! Do anything you like with me, but no pictures.'

To my vast relief she gave a solemn nod and put the phone away.

'Fair enough. I was going to print one out and have it framed for you, as a reminder of your punishment, but perhaps it would be a little too risky. So then, what shall I do with you?'

'You ... you could, maybe, spank me in my nappy and make me kneel for you, still like this. I feel so ashamed of myself, Adrienne, just to be like this, and to be spanked –'

'Would be appropriate, but perhaps rather too much fun for you, and besides, I'd have to pull your nappy down to get at your bottom and that would spoil the effect, or …'

She trailed off, her grin pure cruelty as she approached the bed once more, snapping out an order.

'On your back, Lucy, it's time you were changed, and time you were spanked.'

I lay down, shaking violently at the appalling humili-ation of what was being done to me as my skirt was tugged up once more and my legs lifted to put me into the nappy-changing position. More than one person has spanked me that way, and it has to be about the most shameful, exposed position there is, with the unfortunate girl's legs rolled high to show off every detail of her cunt and well-spread bottom cheeks – but I'd never had it done to me while I was actually in a nappy.

Adrienne was as cool as ever, casually pulling my panties up my legs and twisting them in her fist at the level of my ankles to hold me in position while she pulled open the knots at my hips. With my nappy loose she tugged the front out from under the waistband of my skirt and turned it down on the bed, to leave me bare once more. I had everything showing, every little tuck and fold of my pussy, every tiny wrinkle of my bottom hole, blatantly displayed, and yet with the towelling still against my skin I couldn't forget that I was still in nappies.

I'd thought she'd just spank me, which would have been bad enough, but she was determined to make my ordeal as humiliating as possible. She made a quick trip to the bathroom and came back with powder and cream, hauled my legs up to spread me out once more, sprinkled the powder over my bottom and pussy, then applied cream to my anus and the slit of my cunt. When she touched my clit I nearly came, my back arching and my muscles squeezing tight, but she merely turned her attention back to my bottom hole, sliding one finger deep in up the creamy little ring. A moan escaped my lips as my anus tightened on her finger, which earned me a tut of disapproval and a rebuke.

'You dirty girl, Lucy. Can't you control yourself at all, even when you're having your nappy changed?'

Her finger was still deep in up my bottom and I shook my head, acknowledging the truth of the state I was in, and that whatever she'd done to me it was ultimately my own choice and my own fault. Just two hours before I'd been giving a performance review to a group of managers, most of them older than me, and now I was on my back, having my nappy changed, with my girlfriend's finger up my bottom as she tormented me.

'I could make you come so easily, couldn't I, my little piglet, or I could make you beg for release. I could make you go like this all evening, even sleep like this, and you'd do exactly as you were told, wouldn't you? Maybe

I should even send you into work like this, with a note for Monsieur Montesquieu, asking him to take down your nappy and spank you? You'd like that, wouldn't you, Lucy?'

'You bitch!'

'A bitch, am I? Right …'

She had pushed her thumb in up my cunt as she was speaking and was masturbating me in a leisurely, offhand fashion as her words drove my sense of shame ever higher, but at my response she pulled her hand free, wiped it on my panties and began to spank me, slapping my well-spread bottom and the lips of my cunt to set me gasping and moaning on the instant. I had to come, then and there, with the appalling picture she'd created fresh in my head. My hand went down between my thighs and I was rubbing at my clit while she continued to spank me, laughing all the while at my helpless excitement.

'That's my girl, that's my little piglet. Do it, rub your dirty little cunt while you think about the state you're in, in a nappy, Lucy, and I know what you're thinking about too. You're thinking about having big, bad Monsieur Montesquieu spank your naughty bottom at the office, with your nappy pulled down at the back and your creamy little bumhole ready for his fat old cock, aren't you!'

Suddenly there was anger in her voice, maybe mock, maybe real, but I was already starting to come and couldn't hold back my words.

'Yes, just like that, in my nappy, in front of everybody, then with it pulled down at the back, and he'd fuck me, and bugger me, and make me suck his cock, and spank me and spank me and spank me!'

I screamed, every muscle in my body locked tight as I came under my own fingers, with Adrienne now slapping hard across my open cheeks and on the lips of my cunt, viciously hard smacks I barely felt in my ecstasy.

'I'd do it too, you little bitch,' she spat out, 'but learn this, Lucy. I choose who gets to do dirty things to you – me, Adrienne Vauligneau, and that includes what you think. Now lick my cunt.'

She gave me a last furious salvo of spanks before letting go of my panties and climbing onto the bed. I was still coming, and spread my thighs wide to my fingers even as she straddled my body. My mouth opened wide as she tugged up the tight black dress she was wearing and pulled her panties aside to present me with her naked cunt. I was licking immediately, pathetically grateful for what she'd done to me and more than happy to oblige her in any way she pleased.

My orgasm had begun to fade, but I stayed as I was, my legs wide, my fingers stroking at my pussy and the hot red skin of my cheeks, my bottom wriggling in my open nappy, revelling in my own shame as I licked my mistress to ecstasy. She wasn't exactly gentle about it, grinding her cunt against my mouth and calling me a bitch and slut as I struggled to lick her properly, and also telling me that I belonged to her, over and over again, as she came to her own climax under my eager tongue.

Even then she wasn't done, but rolled me onto my front for a dozen firm swats with my own hairbrush before ordering me to strip. I was made to put my nappy back on as before and serve her dinner like that, in the nude but for the puffy white towelling encasing my hips and bottom and belly, then to get down on my knees and kiss her boots before apologising for my wayward behaviour in fantasising about somebody other than her.

Chapter Three

I had a problem, but it wasn't one I was particularly eager to fix. Adrienne was just too good, with an extraordinary ability to strike to the heart of my sexuality and the strength to stop me backing out when my feelings began to get stronger than I might otherwise have been able to handle. Putting me in a nappy had brought out my feelings of sexual shame in a new and delightful way, while spanking me in that awful, humiliating position had been the final, perfect touch. The episode had also established a wonderful intimacy between us, as we now shared a secret sufficiently taboo to shock all but the most debauched.

That was the good side. The bad side was that she had assumed ownership of me, so fast and so completely that I'd missed my opportunity for the very necessary heart-to-heart talk we should have had on our first day together. I hadn't even told her I had a boyfriend back in London, Magnus, and, although we agreed to a fully open relationship while I was in France, he was sure to visit. So was Stacey, who'd been keeping my bottom warm for me since shortly after I'd joined the company and would want to continue doing so.

Yet if I did tell Adrienne about all this, I was going to end up with relationship issues – either a discontented partner or an ex living almost next door, an ex who'd spanked me and put me in nappies. That was the last thing I needed, with my job more difficult by the day and the pleasure of coming home to Adrienne ever more important. I meant to tell her on the Saturday but it was a cloudy, cool day and we went shopping instead of sunbathing. Sunday was the same, cuddled up together in bed for most of the morning, and when it brightened up in the early afternoon she suggested walking to the Bois de Boulogne. I knew what that meant, and again it was an irresistible alternative to an upsetting conversation all too likely to turn into a full-blown row.

The first time I'd met Adrienne she'd been with her friend Giselle, who worked in insurance but had a taste for the gothic and darker side of sex, dressing completely in black at the weekends to enjoy watching men being dominated, particularly by other men. She wasn't averse to girls either, and I'd already had my face sat on, but what she really liked was to see a man, the more respectable the better, with another man's cock in his mouth.

Giselle was coming with us and we met in their favourite café in the Rue Poussin, full of nervous excitement as we drank a round of pastis to get up a little Dutch courage. As I knew from Adrienne, the important thing was to go out at dusk rather than after dark, and to stay clear of certain areas. If there were any police around, we were simply three innocent young women out for a walk, as she explained as we made our way up the Route de Boulogne à Passy.

'They're not really concerned with the amateurs, or the locals, more the reputation of the area for sex tourism. Still, we have to go a little way in, because I think we ought to introduce Lucy to a Brazilian, don't you, Giselle?'

'Yes, a big one. I'll call Sabrina.'

I began to speak, already feeling as if I was a toy for their amusement and not quite ready for it, but then went quiet, telling myself I'd get the best experience by letting them take control. A brief phone call and Giselle had arranged something for me, something that set my heart fluttering as we turned in among the bushes, because I had a fairly shrewd idea what they were planning. She made two more calls, leaving me with a serious case of the jitters as I imagined being made to service a string of men.

We'd come to an area of dense undergrowth cut through with a maze of little tracks, but Adrienne and

Giselle seemed to know where they were going, and led me to a place where a huge oak sheltered an area of open grass. Leaning against the tree was a person who could only be Sabrina, well over six feet of improbably voluptuous curves packed into a leopard-print dress and supported by lipstick-pink high heels, with a mane of glossy blonde hair falling almost to her waist. She stepped forward as she saw us.

'Hello, girls, and the new one.' Her voice was deep and rich. 'I thought you said you had a little something for me?'

Adrienne applied a firm pat to the seat of my jeans, sending me a couple of steps forward.

'We do, this. She's called Lucy and she's very English.'

Sabrina had joined us, and to my shock and horror her hand went straight between my legs to squeeze my pussy. Then she stepped back with an arch look, wrinkling her nose.

'Do I smell pussy? I certainly think I felt pussy.'

I was too taken aback to speak, and Giselle was laughing, but Adrienne merely sounded amused.

'Yes, Sabrina, fresh English pussy, and she's yours to play with.'

'Why, thank you. Look up, pretty one.'

She put a finger under my chin, in that same commanding gesture Adrienne so often used, and tilted my head up to look into her eyes. I could feel myself melting, unable to resist the way they were using me. Sabrina had clearly accepted Adrienne's offer, for her fingers were exploring the contours of my hips and bottom, my waist and breasts, as she looked down at me. Her gaze had me mesmerised, and even as she hauled up my top to bare my breasts to the cool evening air I couldn't find the will to resist, but put my hands on my head to make them lift and give her full, easy access.

'Perky little thing, aren't you? And such stiff nipples, like little corks.'

Her hands were cupping my breasts, her thumbs making circles around my nipples, bringing both teats to erection and making me whimper in response, then cry out as she ducked down to take one between her teeth. I closed my eyes, lost in shame and ecstasy, and it wasn't until I opened them again that I realised we were no longer alone. Two men had come into the clearing, one small and dapper, one plump and curiously soft-looking, but both so diffident in their manner that I wasn't even alarmed, just increasingly ashamed of myself. Giselle make quick introductions.

'These are Guignol and the Flea, both old friends who'll do exactly as they're told. Kneel, the pair of you.'

Both men knelt in the wet grass without hesitation and Giselle went over to them, while Adrienne barely acknowledged them and Sabrina continued her exploration of my body.

'Top off, I think. Let's have you properly bare.'

My T-shirt was hauled off over my head and I was left topless. Sabrina nodded as I put my hands back on top of my head.

'Very perky, and very obedient. Wherever did you find her?'

Adrienne pushed a hand between my legs from behind as she replied. 'Last month. We caught her peeping at us, so now she's mine. I call her Cochonette.'

'What a naughty girl. I hope you gave her a good spanking?'

A powerful shiver passed through my body at the crucial word and Sabrina laughed. 'Oh, my, she's one of those is she? Does Cochonette like her little piggy bottom spanked?'

She was speaking right into my face, her finger under my chin once more, her tone full of mocking laughter. My blushes must have been enough to give her the answer and I couldn't bring myself to make the awful admission, but Adrienne stepped in.

'She likes to be punished, yes, but it's better to whip her, or she'll enjoy it too much. Come along now, Lucy, where are your manners? I'm sure Sabrina would like to see what you've got packed into those skintight jeans.'

I hesitated and glanced at the two men kneeling beside Giselle, but they were both looking at the ground and seemed to have been ordered not to watch. It gave me an odd feeling of power, for all that I'd been ordered to take my jeans down in front of them. My hands went to my fly, popped the button and eased down the zip, but before I could wriggle my jeans down over my hips Adrienne took hold, stuck her thumbs down the waistband and gave a single sharp tug. I gasped as it all came down, jeans and panties too, down over my hips and lower still, into a tangle at my knees, leaving my bottom and pussy naked as well as my breasts. Sabrina ducked down as Adrienne spoke.

'Hands on your head, Cochonette. Be a good girl and open your legs.'

'Yes, M'selle Adrienne. Oh!'

She slipped her hand back between my thighs to ease one long finger in up my cunt, making me squeak. Meanwhile Sabrina was inspecting my pussy from a distance of inches and breathing in the scent of my excited sex.

'Ah, pussy, so good.'

I cried out again as she pressed her face to my flesh, licking in my slit to tease between my lips and on my clitoris, while Adrienne's fingers still worked in my hole to let my juice out between my legs. Giselle was now holding the plump man, Guignol, by the hair, tipping his head back as if she was forcing him to watch. He looked as frightened as he did excited, but I could feel his eyes on me, lingering over every naked, private curve of my body. He was somehow far more intrusive than the others, more than any ordinary man. The other, the Flea, was still looking at the ground, but he lifted his head slightly to take a surreptitious peek as I was molested in front of him, which Sabrina noticed.

'I think the boys are beginning to get horny, Giselle. Why don't you be nice and let them wank?'

Giselle responded with a sharp slap to Guignol's face and a brief, stern order that had both men scrabbling to get their cocks out. Guignol was already hard, but tiny, with a stubby pink prick that barely stuck out of his hand as he took hold and began to masturbate. The Flea was more impressive, stroking a big, surprisingly dark cock, still flaccid but with the head beginning to poke out from the foreskin. I wondered if I'd be made to suck them, even let them fuck me, an almost impossibly humiliating prospect when both were so lacking in virility, yet I knew I'd accept, spread out on my back or kneeling to let them in from behind while the others looked on and laughed. Adrienne seemed to sense my thoughts.

'I'm not sure the little toads are capable of actually fucking a woman, Lucy, but somebody else is, aren't you, darling?'

She was talking to Sabrina, who nodded, stood up and in the same motion pushed me down to my knees. I'd guessed the truth from the start, but that didn't ease my feelings much as she tugged up her dress to reveal a pair of tiny pink nylon panties, not smooth over the triangle of a pussy but bulging with a heavy, dark cock and a pair of truly monstrous balls. She, or he, was already half stiff, the cock stirring beneath the see-through panties. Instinctively my mouth opened and my hand reached out, first to squeeze it all through the tarty nylon knickers, then to pull them down at the front, flopping everything out as Adrienne gave a soft, breathless order.

'Get sucking, Cochonette ... no, kiss her cock first, just to show your appreciation.'

I looked up at Adrienne, half hoping she'd let me off, half hoping she'd grab me by the hair and force my face against Sabrina's crotch, but all I got was a hard, cruel stare. Sabrina put a hand down to cup her cock and balls, offering it all to my mouth, and before I really knew what I was doing I'd puckered up and planted a single neat kiss on the very tip. Adrienne gave a pleased chuckle and cuffed me gently across the back of my head, encouraging me to take in Sabrina's cock and suck. I do love a nice big cock in my mouth, and this was no exception, despite the shame of being made to do it with everybody watching.

Guignol actually looked sorry for me, the Flea more jealous, although both were wanking at the sight of me moving my lips back and forth along Sabrina's rapidly stiffening shaft. Giselle was paying more attention to the men than to me, but Adrienne was grinning, thoroughly enjoying the view and plainly aroused for all her cool exterior. Sabrina had given a soft, pleased moan as I took her in, and now she spoke with the same happy but assertive tone as before.

'That is nice. What a good little cocksucker you are, Lucy. And now, how about a little attention to my balls?'

I obliged, taking her cock in my hand as I pushed my face closer still to lick and kiss the huge, heavy ball sac, provoking a fresh moan from Adrienne.

'She loves her cock, too much really,' she said. 'I had to whip her for sucking off lorry drivers the other day.'

'Oh, my, what a dirty girl. You like them big and rough, do you, Lucy?'

I was licking at the underside of her balls and merely nodded my confession as Adrienne carried on.

'Big anyway. She fancies her boss too, and he's anything but rough, just an old roué, but she doesn't care. She was fantasising over being spanked by him in front of the rest of the office.'

I glanced up briefly, shaking my head, desperate not to have my already burning shame made worse by a description of the nappy incident. Adrienne winked and cuffed me back into position, and I took Sabrina's now fully erect cock back into my mouth as she stroked my hair. I usually like to close my eyes when I'm sucking cock, but this was different. The way Sabrina's erection and balls thrust up out of the little pink panties was strangely compelling, obscene and yet fascinating, as were the exaggerated curves of her figure, especially her pair of heavy breasts. She saw my interest and spoke to Adrienne.

'I do believe the little tart wants to see my boobies. Here we are then, doll.'

She pulled up her dress, baring first a big lacy bra in the same cheap pink nylon as her knickers, then two huge, round breasts, fat and heavy, almost grotesquely feminine, like some bizarre parody of the female form. Yet she was right, I did want to see, and my sucking immediately grew more urgent as I imagined how it would feel to be suckled at her breast, preferably after a good hard spanking, a thought at once appalling and compelling.

I wasn't the only one who liked the view. Both men were now hammering on their cocks with their eyes fixed on Sabrina, my own dirty behaviour and humiliation no more than detail. Guignol began to beg, incoherent words tumbling from his mouth as his gaze flicked up to Giselle then back to Sabrina and me, while the Flea looked as if he was about to cry for sheer jealousy, though he continued to wank furiously. Sabrina laughed.

'I do believe the boys want a suck. Shall I be kind?'

She didn't wait for an answer but pulled back to leave me gaping and dizzy in reaction to her monstrous cock. She stepped across to the two men. At Giselle's instructions they were made to beg, each putting up his hands as if he were a puppy, before being allowed to take Sabrina's erection into their mouths. I guessed they normally had to pay for the privilege, and both were in ecstasy from the start, Guignol with his eyes closed in bliss as he mouthed Sabrina's erection and the Flea with his tongue hanging out and his eyes burning with need.

They looked ridiculous, both utterly robbed of their masculinity as they sucked on a shemale's cock and masturbated at the pleasure of it, but I was no better, pathetically grateful for getting the treatment myself and desperately in need of more. I want her to spank me, suckle me, fuck me, anything she wanted to do as long as it involved my body being well and truly used, and all in front of Adrienne and Giselle before I gave them their pleasure in turn.

I was barely aware that I'd slipped a hand between my thighs and begun to masturbate, showing no more dignity than the two men, but I no longer cared, They'd put me where I belonged, on my knees with my mouth full of the taste of cock, topless and with my jeans and panties in a tangle halfway down my legs. Adrienne noticed, took me firmly by the hair and pulled my face into her crotch so that I could nuzzle her through her jeans as she masturbated. I could have come like that, so easily, but Giselle wasn't done. Laughing, she made a suggestion that brought me out of my erotic trance with a jerk.

'Let's make Lucy suck the boys. Now that would be funny.'

Adrienne gave her soft, cruel chuckle and I knew it was pointless to protest, even before she clicked her finger and pointed to where Sabrina had just transferred her cock to the Flea's mouth.

'Crawl over, get sucking.'

I began, only to find my legs tangled in my jeans and panties, which I quickly stripped off along with my shoes. Now stark naked, I crawled over towards the two men as Giselle ordered them to rock back on their heels, presenting their cocks. I couldn't even look Guignol in the eye as I went down on him and took his cock as deep as it would go while he squeezed and stroked his balls. Adrienne laughed and planted a firm slap across my raised bottom.

'How does that feel, Lucy, with that little toad's prick in your mouth, just like he was a real man? Now the Flea.'

Her fingers tightened in my hair as she finished speaking and I was pulled up by main force and swung over to take in the Flea's much bigger cock. He immediately begun to fuck in my mouth, making me gag and clutch at the grass as Giselle took her turn to spank me, calling me a slut and a tart as her palm slapped down across my naked bottom. I put my hand back, lost in shame, and began to masturbate once more, only for Sabrina to speak up.

'That I have to fuck, if I may, Adrienne?'

I knew what 'that' was my upturned bottom. My wet, open cunt was on show and an invitation to any cock, but so was my bumhole, no doubt tight and maybe equally inviting. There was no way I could possibly accommodate her enormous penis up my bottom and I pulled back immediately, gabbling urgently to Sabrina as she got behind me.

'You can fuck me, but not up my bottom, please.'

She just laughed.

'Who said anything about your bottom, you dirty bitch? Now get back down on his cock.'

Adrienne still had me by the hair and immediately thrust my head back down on the Flea's erection, forcing me to suck him once more even as Sabrina's cock head pressed against my pussy hole. I felt her go up and I was full at both ends, spit-roasted in a public park, naked and humiliated, with a cock in my mouth and a cock up my cunt, and masturbating over my own filthy behaviour as they used me. Sabrina's huge balls were slapping on my hand, the Flea's cock was so far down my throat I was starting to choke, both Adrienne and Giselle were laughing at me ... it was just perfect, a situation at once so awful, so unbearably shameful and so utterly exquisite that with a few more firm touches to my clitoris I tipped myself over the edge.

I came, and as my body went tight on their erections,

so did they, almost together, the Flea's cock jetting sperm down my throat an instant before Sabrina whipped hers free to spunk all over my bottom. Even that didn't stop me, and my fingers were still busy with my now aching cunt as I gobbled on the Flea's cock and Sabrina wiped hers over my cheeks and in my slit, deliberately soiling me before snatching at my hair to pull me around and jam herself deep into my throat.

When she let go I just collapsed, to lie filthy and exhausted in the wet grass, but so happy I was laughing, utterly indifferent to the state I was in or where I was. My thighs were wide to the low evening sun, my hands on my boobs and my hair spread out on the grass. I was completely content but happy to be used in any way the rest of them pleased, which was just as well.

Guignol had come in his hand as he watched me used, and he and the Flea were quickly sent packing, while Sabrina was told to stand guard while Adrienne and Giselle had their fun with me. I didn't mind, far from it, only too eager to please as Giselle planted one foot on either side of my head and made a neat curtsey over my face. She was in long, loose skirts with petticoats underneath but no knickers, so I was left unable to see and with a faceful of fanny.

I did my best to be a good girl, licking earnestly at her cunt until she began to sigh and then to moan. Adrienne had got hold of my ankles and rolled my legs up into

47

the same shameful position as when she'd spanked me on the Friday night, but this time she eased her fingers into my cunt and tickled my bottom hole as I licked at Giselle, who was soon crying out in ecstasy as she rubbed herself against my face.

She'd no sooner climbed off than Adrienne replaced her, with a quick, cautious glance around the clearing before she squatted down, presenting me with the seat of her jeans, just inches from my face. I knew what she was going to do, even before she had pushed down her jeans and panties to bare her cunt and her little round bottom. Sure enough, she sat down as if she was on the loo, with her cheeks spread wide over my face.

'Kiss it, Cochonette, kiss my anus.'

I did it, too far gone to stop myself, with Giselle and Sabrina looking on as I planted a firm kiss on my lover's neat, velvet-smooth bottom hole. Without needing further orders, I began to lick. Adrienne responded with a happy sigh and wriggled her bottom down onto my face, so that my tongue was well in up her bumhole. She slipped a hand between her legs, and as she began to masturbate I told myself that, whatever happened, I very definitely did not want to lose her.

Chapter Four

One way or another, I had to tell Adrienne about Magnus and Stacey. I also had to establish some ground rules for our relationship that went beyond me being her sex toy. I meant to do it as we were walking back from the Bois de Boulogne, but we were still tidying up when Sabrina got a call to say there was a police van in the little car park at the end of the Route de Boulogne à Passy. It wasn't quite dark, and Adrienne and I were safe enough, but Giselle less so in her black outfit and Sabrina not at all.

We split up, Adrienne and I walking ahead and phoning back to the others from time to time to make sure they got clear, which left all four of us laughing and well pleased with ourselves by the time we'd come out into Boulogne-Billancourt. I was pleased to find that, despite the way I'd grovelled to all three, both Giselle and Sabrina treated me as an equal once the play was over. Adrienne was rather different, making a point of displaying her dominance, and clearly showing off to her friends. I didn't mind, but it wasn't the moment to start a serious conversation, and by the time we'd shared a meal and returned to the Rue de la Cure by taxi I was too tired.

Monday was exceptionally busy, with several of the staff seemingly determined to test my authority, while M. Montesquieu didn't come in at all. By the time I left I was in a mood to tackle a dozen Adriennes and had to stop for a glass of wine in order to calm down a little. I'd decided to be completely honest and deal with any questions or objections she had as they came up, then offer her the chance to punish me in any way she felt fit in order to make up for my behaviour. Not that I'd done anything wrong, but it would make her feel better, and, after all, it was central to our relationship that I should be punished.

She wasn't in her apartment, but a delicious aroma was leaking from the oven and the living-room window was open. I climbed out onto the leads, to find her much as I'd expected, lying face-down on a towel with nothing on but a pair of minuscule black bikini pants. Her bottom made a very inviting target indeed, but I managed to resist the temptation of announcing my arrival with a slap to her near-naked cheeks, and called out instead. She stirred, turned and adjusted her shades so that she could look at me from over the top.

'Oh, there you are, Lucy. Strip off and join me.'

'I'll go and get changed then.'

'No, just go in, strip off and come back out with the bottle of Riesling you'll find in the fridge and two glasses.'

I hesitated, quite keen on the idea of taking off all my clothes then and there, but also quite keen on a brief shower first, while there was an obvious drawback to going fully nude. We were in plain view of the flats at the back, and on a balcony almost directly opposite us was an elderly man with an unmistakably military bearing, presumably the old soldier Adrienne had mentioned before. The situation provided the perfect excuse to assert myself.

'I really need a shower, and my bikini, or at very least the bottoms.'

'Don't be such a prude, Lucy. Now strip.'

'What about Commandant Arnauld?'

'Don't be ungracious. He likes to watch, and as far as I'm concerned he's earned the privilege. Besides, he won't see anything I wouldn't be prepared to show on a beach.'

'Yes, but he's actually watching, right now.'

'Of course he is. I told him we'd be out on the roof, and that you'd be nude.'

'Adrienne!'

Even as she spoke he gave us a cheerful wave, then raised his glass in salute. Another man had come out as well, much younger, with a lean, tanned body but with enough height and muscle to appeal to my taste, which immediately made the idea of sunbathing in the nude

51

both more attractive and more embarrassing. Adrienne had ignored my shocked response on discovering that she'd more or less invited a voyeur to enjoy watching me nude, but now she indicated the younger man.

'That's his grandson, Marcelon. Now surely you don't mind stripping off in front of him?'

'That's not really the point, Adrienne ...'

'Come on, silly, we're not in London now, you know. Clothes off, or do I have to take them off for you, and maybe give you a jolly good over-the-knee, bare-bottom spanking, in front of both of them?'

She'd said the crucial words in English, deliberately mocking me and my love of having my bottom smacked by hand and over the knee, which she considered both very funny and very British. I went red straightaway, but managed to stick my tongue out at her before ducking back inside, sure that I'd earned myself a punishment, and probably quite a severe one, but determined to get my way. I'd also judged that she wouldn't follow me indoors, so I took my time as I undressed and used her shower, then rummaged through her drawers until I found another bikini. It was less revealing than the one she had on, but a bit small for me, leaving more bottom cheek showing than I'd normally have chosen, and quite tricky to do up behind my back, but it did at least cover me.

I also had the perfect lead into my little speech, I was very sure indeed that she wasn't physically capable of spanking me against my will, even in the unlikely event of her trying. Admittedly, it was rather nice to imagine her taking me forcibly across her knee, there on the roof, in full view of both Commandant Arnauld and his nephew, with my bikini bottoms hauled down and my bare cheeks turning a glowing red. I'd even have got off on it, but there's a time and a place, so if she wanted to punish me she would at least have to wait until I'd had my say.

Her eyebrows rose as I climbed up to join her on the leads, and there was steel in her voice as she addressed me.

'I hope you're planning to take that bikini off, Lucy?'

'No, not in front of them.'

'Why not? Because you haven't been introduced? You weren't so precious in front of Guignol and the Flea, and look at them! At least Marcelon's got a good body, and old man Arnauld must have been very attractive in his day.'

'That's beside the point, Adrienne. Look, we need to talk.'

'We do, about your persistent disobedience.'

'Maybe later. The thing is, I really enjoy the way you are with me, but you rather took me by surprise, that first day, so I didn't have a chance to explain how things are back in London.'

She immediately looked annoyed, and there was jealousy in her voice as she replied, 'Who is it, some English bitch who's been attending to your bottom, or some hulking lorry driver who's going to come over and expect to fuck you in his cab?'

'That's not fair, Adrienne ... OK, it's not that far from the truth. I'm in an open relationship with a man called Magnus. He's so big, he looks like a Viking, and –'

'He drives a lorry?'

'No, he deals in luxury spirits, malt whisky, cognac, that sort of thing. There's Stacey too, she ... she attends to my bottom, I suppose you could say.'

'And you want her to be able to continue to attend to your bottom, and to go to bed with this Viking boy? You're a greedy slut, Lucy, what are you?'

'A greedy slut, if you say so, but ...'

'So why can't you get rid of them? You live in Paris now, and you're mine. You do want to be mine, don't you?'

'Yes, of course, but after all, you don't mind me going with other people, do you?'

'When it's my choice, no, but it has to be my choice.'

'Sorry.'

She looked upset, and I'd said all I could think of to say, so I put a hand out and stroked her shoulder, waiting for her to speak. Across the gardens Commandant Arnauld and his grandson were still watching us and drinking their wine, no doubt imagining some light-hearted, playful conversation. I was wishing they'd go in, especially if Adrienne and I were about to have a blazing row, but when she finally twisted around to speak to me her voice was level, if not actually happy.

'OK, I understand. After all, I wouldn't want you going off somewhere and texting me the next day to say somebody else had taken charge of you. You can sleep with your Viking, when he visits, and if I approve of him who knows? Maybe we can even introduce him to a few friends. As for Stacey, what's she like?'

'She's lovely, very calm and thoughtful, naturally strong, but not cruel, not like you.'

'But she punishes you?'

'Yes, but playfully. She likes to spank me, but she's not a natural.'

'Is she attractive?'

'She's tall, with dark hair, very athletic. She'd like you.'

I was actually fairly sure that Stacey would think Adrienne an unspeakable little brat, but it seemed better to suggest they'd get on, especially if they weren't likely to meet. She paused to think once more, frowning, then nodded.

'OK, if she visits, she can play with you, as long as you make it very clear that I'm in charge, got it?'

'Yes. Thank you, that's really sweet of you. I was so scared you wouldn't understand.'

'I understand you, Lucy, maybe better than you do yourself. Now get that bikini off.'

'Yes, Adrienne.'

I didn't really have much choice, but that only made my embarrassment worse as I undid my top and pulled it off, then slipped my bikini bottoms down my legs, while the two men watched and grinned with delight to see me strip. Now nude, I laid out my towel, then hesitated, conscious that if I lay down beside Adrienne I'd be giving them a fine view of my bare bottom, with a very high risk of flashing my pussy, and yet it seemed silly to lie head to tail. Unable to make a decision, I knelt down instead, sideways on so that they could only really see my boobs, and poured some sunblock onto Adrienne's back to give myself an excuse not to lie down. She didn't seem to realise my dilemma, but sighed happily as I began to massage the cream into her shoulders, and when she spoke again her voice was once more relaxed.

'Good girl. You do realise that you're going to have to be punished, don't you?'

'Yes, of course.'

'And I want you to promise me that you'll do as you're told in future. Other than Stacey and the Viking, you're mine, completely, to do with as I please.'

'Yes, Adrienne, except for anything that might make me lose my job, or leave permanent marks, or –'

'I know the score, Lucy, although I admit I am tempted to have your cunt tattooed.'

'Sorry, but ...'

'You are being a little madam today, aren't you? OK, if

that's the way you want it, you can have a choice: either a neat little tattoo on your cunt, just on the mound, maybe "Property of Adrienne Vauligneau", or perhaps just plain "Cochonette". Yes, that would be perfect, because whatever happens you'll always know you're a piglet.'

'That's sweet, and I would enjoy it, but I really don't want to be marked. What's the alternative?'

'To go to bed with Marcelon.'

* * *

I can think of worse things than being fucked by a stalwart Frenchman, for all the shame of being given to him as if I was a doll to be passed around for amusement. That was what I liked about the situation anyway, but Adrienne didn't have my deep-seated hang-ups about sex, and that made me rather suspicious. After all, all she'd really done, however we dressed it up, was set me up on a date with Marcelon. How could that be a punishment?

Admittedly I knew I'd get fucked, which isn't normal on conventional dates, but I knew equally well that if I decided I really didn't want it I'd be able to turn him down. Bearing that in mind, as I made my way north on the Metro, I was wondering what she'd told him. He was a big man, and if he'd been told he could spank me I was in trouble. The thought frightened me and made me weak at the knees with arousal, all at the same time.

I knew I'd give in to it, though, and by the time I arrived at the Grésillons stop, I was already imagining how I'd feel once I was panties-down across his knee with his huge hand rising and falling upon my bottom.

I was supposed to meet him directly after work, so I was still in my office suit and feeling out of place and slightly insecure. The district, Gennevilliers, was very different from the 16th arrondissement, outside the Périphérique for one thing, and so not really in Paris at all, at least as Adrienne thought of it. The Avenue de Grésillons, where he worked, was lined with blocks of flats and rather seedy-looking shops, while the side streets looked worse, with many of the buildings in a state of decay.

The address Adrienne had given me turned out to be a butcher's shop, and I wondered if she was playing some sort of joke on me, until Marcelon himself came out onto the pavement. He looked even bigger than I remembered him, well over six foot, and broad-shouldered into the bargain, an image of crude strength made stronger still by his blood-spattered apron and the cleaver he held in one huge hand, still smeared with bits of whatever he'd been chopping.

He'd only come out for a cigarette, but noticed me immediately and recognised me. I blushed, remembering that the last time he'd seen me I'd been stark naked and massaging sunblock into my girlfriend's back. His grin said it all, but I managed a smile in return, at which he made a gesture with one hand and disappeared back into the shop. He returned a moment later with a large, curiously squashy-looking parcel.

'Andouillette, hand-made.'

'Thank you.'

I'd have preferred flowers, or perhaps a few good chocolates, but he obviously meant well and I tried to look pleased as I examined the dozen fat, oblong sausages he'd given me. He seemed happy with my reaction and immediately took my hand. Then, after speaking briefly to somebody inside the shop, he set off down the street with me in tow. I was still holding the packet of andouil-lette and couldn't help but feel slightly silly, if no longer insecure, not with a man like him beside me, although he had at least left his meat cleaver in the shop.

He was still in his overalls though, and as we walked I caught the faint tang of fresh blood mixed with fresh masculine sweat, an earthy combination that had me even more flustered than I'd anticipated. I wondered if he was simply going to take me back to his house and fuck me then and there, and afterwards perhaps make me cook the andouillette for dinner, but to my surprise, after we'd gone only a couple of hundred yards, he pushed open the door of a bar.

They knew him, and greeted him with cheerful salutes and not a few remarks on his company. One enormously fat man with a bristly moustache asked if he'd been fishing, as he'd obviously made a good catch. Another, a man like a weasel, made a far from complimentary remark about mackerel, but Marcelon told him to shut up. Then he introduced me, and after that they were at least friendly, although every one of them seemed to be undressing me with his eyes.

We ate steak, which was very good indeed, served with fries and washed down with strong, rough red wine from a carafe that must have held two litres. I took my share, eager to calm my nerves for what was coming, because Marcelon's behaviour left no doubt at all of his intentions: he expected to fuck me. The prurient interest of his friends suggested that if they didn't know exactly what was going on, they at least had a fair idea. It didn't help that their French was so fast and full of slang expressions that I could barely follow it. Most of their jokes went right over my head, but I understood enough to realise that most of them involved Marcelon and me. I also caught Adrienne's name and more than one reference to nude sunbathing. At that, Marcelon pushed his empty plate away and leant back on the long padded bench we were sitting on.

'She is something else, that one, a real wild cat. She even tells me what to do. Can you believe that?'

The fat man answered him.

'And you let her?'

'I let her. I'll show you why I let her.'

Marcelon was sitting by the window and had leant forward to talk to the fat man, who was propping up the bar with a glass of beer in one hand. I was between them, fiddling with my now empty wine glass and wondering if it would be rude to ask for more, when suddenly, without the slightest warning, Marcelon grabbed me by the hair and hauled me across his legs.

I immediately knew what was going to happen, but all I could manage was a squeal of protest and despair as my office skirt was hauled high to show off the seat of my panties, which were hauled down before I could even make a grab for them, and with that my bottom was bare to the whole place. They were laughing, every one of them, even the two women further along the bar, all finding it absolutely hilarious to watch me get my bottom stripped in a public bar and then be spanked.

This was my punishment, a public spanking, bare bottom and in front of complete strangers, administered by a man who not only was as strong as an ox and utterly oblivious to my dignity but really knew how to spank a girl. I was squealing like a pig from the first slap, at least when I could get enough air into my lungs to squeal at all, and when I started to kick my feet in reaction to the pain he simply hooked one massive leg around my thigh to keep me in place – and in doing so spread my naked cunt to the entire bar.

That really raised a laugh, and there was another as my panties ripped, leaving my free and now shoe-less leg kicking wildly in the air as the smacks continued to rain down. It wasn't just my pussy on show but my bumhole too as Marcelon adjusted his grip to spread me out into a yet ruder position. The fat man made some dirty remark about what he could see and how wet I was, while one of the women told me to stop being such a baby, and still Marcelon spanked. My bottom bounced to the slaps and my cheeks were so hot that it felt as if my skin was on fire.

They were no hotter than my face, though. The shame of a public spanking was raging in my head, despite the pain of what was being done to my bottom. But even as I blubbered and howled my feelings, I was aware of what the rough treatment was doing to me. I'd be masturbating over the experience for years, but that didn't help at all while it was happening, nor when it finally stopped and I lay panting across Marcelon's knee with my legs still cocked wide to leave my sopping cunt open for easy inspection.

He was holding me around the waist and still had one of my legs trapped. I could feel the hard bump of his cock pressing into my side, and wondered if I was simply to be fucked then and there, over the table with my body thrust down on the dirty plates and spilt wine. I'd have taken it too, but he had something worse in store for me – one of the andouillettes, inserted into my open cunt with a soft, wet squelching noise that once more set the entire bar laughing.

'That was her punishment,' he said, 'for wanting to fuck an Englishman – the spanking, not the andouillette up her hole. That's just to keep her open for something bigger.'

There was more laughter and he finally released me, allowing me to get to my feet and tug my skirt down. My bottom was on fire, my panties a ruined rag around one ankle, so I abandoned them on the floor. But I wasn't even given a chance to sort myself out – Marcelon simply took me by the hand and led me away, while I was still trying to get my skirt down over my bare red bottom. Ignoring my snivelling and my rather feeble protests, he led me further along the street and then into the Rue François Kovac, a street even more run-down than the others. His apartment was in a block halfway along, and I was led upstairs and told to undress. He watched as I stripped, his cock already out, a great thick pole of meat protruding from his open fly above a heavily wrinkled ball sac, which I was ordered to lick as soon as I was nude.

I did it kneeling, caressing my hot bottom as I flicked my tongue over the musky flesh, and he masturbated as he watched. My thoughts were a mess, but gradually coming together, with one thing more important than any other. I'd been spanked in public, hard and on my bare bottom, something so good, so impossibly shameful and so exquisitely desirable that it hurt just to think about it. He'd given me a bare-bottom spanking in front of his laughing friends, my cunt and anus on show and my cheeks bouncing and spreading to the slaps, unable to stop it and unable to protect myself.

He put his cock in my mouth as I began to fuck myself with the andouillette, sliding the fat pale sausage in and out of my slippery little hole as I mouthed and kissed his magnificent erection, saying, 'Thank you for my spanking' the way a girl ought to, with a slow, loving blowjob. I'd have taken him all the way too, and happily swallowed or even let him do it in my face, but that wasn't what he wanted.

I was turned around and pushed down over the sofa with my smacked bottom sticking up in the air, the andouillette was pulled from my pussy and stuck in my mouth, then I was fucked. His rock-hard stomach was slapping on my well-smacked bottom cheeks as he pumped into me, the perfect reminder of what he'd done to me as I rubbed my greedy little cunt to an orgasm so strong it brought me to the edge of blacking out.

Chapter Five

Sometimes, the more you want to gain, the more you have to surrender. Hold back and you live your life in grey, safe respectability, but give in to what you really need and every moment becomes an exquisite thrill. I'd given up my privacy, my dignity, my right to the control of my own body, but in return for constant, breathless excitement so strong that it took real effort to calm it so that I could do my work. Fortunately I'm rather good at that, after years of maintaining my good reputation while getting up to all sorts of naughty behaviour in my private moments.

On the morning after my punishment from Marcelon I arrived at work at the usual time and as smart as ever, save for my missing panties, despite having spent most of the night being fucked by a fervent Frenchman. I was a little tired but no more, and my efforts at asserting myself seemed to be bearing fruit, as most of the staff were getting on with what they were supposed to do without constantly trying to challenge me. Even M. Montesquieu was being helpful, staying at his desk until nearly one o'clock and signing off the changes I'd made to office practice.

I wanted to tell Adrienne what had happened, perhaps with a carefully phrased email to say that I had been punished and accepted the necessity of what had been done to me. Unfortunately it was out of the question. I held ultimate responsibility for monitoring the office's internet access, and it would have been wrong to abuse the system; besides, one of the geeks in IT was sure to catch me out. I contented myself with a text, saying simply, 'It's been dealt with, thank you,' which I hoped would strike the right note.

She didn't reply, and after that I forced myself to concentrate solely on work. I was feeling that I'd put in a good day when M. Montesquieu called me into his office. The last time I'd seen him he'd been rolling gently down the corridor with lunch on his mind, and I hadn't even realised he was back. He'd certainly been doing himself well: his big, rosy face was beaded with sweat as he beamed at me from behind his desk.

'Ah, M'selle Salisbury ... Lucinda, I just wanted to tell you what an excellent job you've been doing. Just a few weeks ago the place seemed moribund. I thought it was the end, but you have us buzzing like a hive of bees. Would you care to dine with me tonight, at L'Alsacien perhaps, if that's to your taste? It would be my little thank-you, and a way to get to know you better.'

I was surprised, as until then he'd seemed to take my presence completely for granted, and I was wishing he'd given me a little more notice, but it seemed impolitic to refuse. 'Thank you, M. Montesquieu, yes, that would be delightful,' I answered cautiously. I was determined to keep our relationship on a strictly professional level despite my fantasies about being taken over his knee for a spanking.

His response was straightforward and friendly, if ever so slightly familiar. 'Excellent, and please do call me Claude, as you are my lieutenant. We officers must stick together.'

I'd had no idea he had a military background, but even as he spoke I realised that the black and white picture of a slender young man in uniform was not some long-dead relative, as I'd supposed, but M. Montesquieu himself. Some sort of comment seemed to be in order.

'Thank you, Claude, although I've never been an officer, or anything of the sort, but I see you have.'

He gave a grave nod at the picture before replying. 'Algeria, 1962. Nasty business.'

I made a hasty calculation and realised that he was even older than I'd thought, well past the age when he could have taken retirement, which went some way to explaining his behaviour. As with Commandant Arnauld and Adrienne, his military background increased my respect for him. I realised it would also give me something to talk about over what might otherwise have been a rather tedious dinner, so I thanked him for the invitation once more and promised to return at six o'clock.

Back in my office I sent Adrienne another text, explaining what was going on and apologising if she'd already bought dinner. Again she didn't reply, making me wonder briefly if she was cross with me for spending the night with Marcelon when she'd only ordered me to be spanked and fucked, but it was far more likely that she simply hadn't bothered to recharge her phone.

The rest of the afternoon passed swiftly, and I was soon on my way to L'Alsacien, which I'd heard was one of the best restaurants in Paris. It was certainly exclusive, and as we climbed out of the cab I was wishing I'd had a chance to change into something more elegant, although as most of the couples dining there seemed to consist of elderly gentlemen escorting much younger women I didn't feel out of place.

M. Montesquieu was well known to the staff, just as Marcelon had been at the bar the night before – an amusing contrast that made me wonder if the guests at L'Alsacien would laugh as loudly at the sight of me being given a bare-bottom spanking by my host. One thing was certain: he wouldn't have to wrestle with his conscience about taking my knickers down, as I didn't have any on, so I took my seat with considerable caution. There were no andouillettes available to stuff up me either, only a range of exquisite delicacies and fine wines, to which M. Montesquieu appeared determined to do full justice.

As the meal progressed his complexion grew ever darker and his manner more effusive, although he was never vulgar nor even suggestive. He was a good conversationalist as well, allowing me to talk when I had something to say, and full of interesting memories and wisdom from a long and eventful life. Soon he was calling me Lucy and I didn't correct him, although I'd always been Lucinda at the office. I found myself liking him more and more, and imagining how it would feel to be put across his knee, especially as, despite my best efforts, the wine was beginning to get to me.

He insisted on a bottle with every course, all of them delicious, and it was impossible not to at least sample them, but the waiters would refill my glass long before it was empty. M. Montesquieu simply soaked it up as if he didn't expect to live to see the dawn, but it didn't seem to make any difference. I managed reasonably well, a benefit of extensive private etiquette lessons which had included discreet advice on how a lady should behave if she inadvertently became inebriated.

Unfortunately my tutors hadn't taken full account of the effects of highly polished marble floors, or of the lady in question going around with no knickers on. I had delayed my trip to the loo as long as possible, and was trying to hurry and concentrate on walking properly at the same time, when the floor seemed to slide away beneath me. I twisted round as I fell and landed on my bottom with my legs apart, facing back towards M. Montesquieu and accidentally treating not only him but two waiters and the people at several nearby tables to a flash of bare blonde pussy. M. Montesquieu was a perfect gentleman and helped me to my feet while managing to keep a straight face, though he'd obviously seen. For myself, I was blushing pink for the rest of the meal, which fortunately wasn't long, and I was very glad indeed to get out of the restaurant and into a taxi.

I knew what was going to happen once I was back at the Rue de la Cure. I couldn't help myself. If Adrienne was awake I'd tell her what had happened, and perhaps admit to my imagined spankings just to make absolutely sure I got punished. If she was asleep I'd just go to my room, lie down on the bed with my legs open and let my imagination take over, leading me down some path of shame-filled fantasy as I masturbated myself to a badly needed orgasm.

Adrienne hadn't replied to any of the increasingly desperate texts I'd sent while I was in the cab, so either her phone was out of action or she'd gone to bed early, but I went up to her apartment anyway. I heard the voices even as I was climbing the stairs, Adrienne's and another, deeper but rich and feminine, which had my pulse running faster still as I pushed my key into the door. Adrienne was standing with her feet braced apart in the middle of the living room, wearing a black see-through peignoir that did more to enhance her slender curves than to conceal them, along with stockings and high heels, while in her hands she held her whip. With her, as I'd guessed, was Sabrina, in nothing but a scarlet corset, with stockings and heels in the same vivid shade, her heavy breasts bare, no panties, her cock sticking up like a flagpole. Adrienne had heard me come in and turned towards me.

'At last, the piglet honours us with her presence. Where have you been, Lucy?'

'I'm sorry, Adrienne, but M. Montesquieu asked me out for dinner. I did text you. Hi, Sabrina.'

Sabrina smiled and wagged a finger at me in mocking admonition, making my cheeks squeeze under my skirt as Adrienne carried on.

'Dinner with M. Montesquieu, was it? That's her boss, Sabrina, the one she'd like to be spanked by. Did he, Lucy?'

'No, of course not ... unfortunately. He's the perfect gentleman, but I did fall over and ... and give him an accidental flash of my pussy. I've got no panties on, you see, because they got ripped when Marcelon spanked me in the bar, in front of everybody, bare, and they all laughed at me, and … and he stuck a sausage up my cunt, and he took me back to his place and fucked me … that was what I deserved, though, all of it. Thank you, M'selle Adrienne.'

It had all come out in a rush, everything I'd wanted to say to her all day, and I hung my head as I finished, praying she'd react as I wanted, with good humour but still finding an excuse to punish me again. She stepped close, lifted my chin with the handle of her dog whip as she liked to do and looked into my eyes.

'So you enjoyed what Marcelon did to you? Yes, I expect you did, rather too much in fact, although he tells me you made a dreadful fuss.'

'It was a genuine punishment, please believe me.'

'I know that, Lucy, because I know the way you think.'

'And he stuck the andouillette up my pussy in the bar, in front of a dozen or so complete strangers who'd been watching me spanked.'

'Yes, he told me, an amusing little detail I hadn't ordered but which I'm prepared to let go. But I'm not sure if I can be so lenient about you spending the night with him. How many times did he fuck you?'

'Um … five, six maybe.'

'Five or six? You dirty, greedy little bitch. Why didn't you come back after two or three?'

I shrugged, unable to provide an excuse. We both knew full well I was in for it whatever I said. Adrienne nodded, turned her back on me and walked towards Sabrina, who'd been nursing her erection as we talked, but quickly moved her hands aside and thrust out her hips. Adrienne extended the dog whip and curled the tip around Sabrina's balls and the shaft of her cock before giving a sudden expert flick. Sabrina gasped and I saw a powerful shudder run through her body as Adrienne resumed.

'Stand in the corner, Lucy, with your skirt turned up and your hands on your head ... no, not with your bottom showing to the room, you little pervert, the other way around. Yes, that's better, and you can open your blouse. Now then, Sabrina was just having her cock whipped, a little treat I give her occasionally, and I don't see why your appearance should be allowed to spoil her fun, so you can watch and wait. I'll deal with you presently. No touching, Sabrina.'

I'd followed her orders, making only one mistake in that I was used to doing corner time with my bottom on show, but with my skirt rucked up and my blouse undone I was in an equally sorry position as Adrienne went back to work. Sabrina already looked fit to burst, her cock so hard that the head was glossy and the veins stood out on the shaft, and as the whip touched her once she gave a another shudder, making her breasts quiver as she pushed herself into a yet more vulnerable position.

Another flick of the whip and Sabrina cried out in ecstasy, but I was sure she'd need to be handled in order to come, maybe sucked, and absolutely certain whose job that was going to be. I wondered if Adrienne would have done it, had I not been there, and that provoked a moment of illicit delight as I imagined her with her cool, haughty face streaked with spunk or her perfectly painted lips agape on Sabrina's massive cock. It wasn't going to happen, but it was nice to imagine it might and then end up having to do it myself … but I'd underestimated Adrienne's skill.

She gave Sabrina's cock and balls a few more precise touches of the dog whip, then made a sudden twirling motion to wrap the fine leather tip around the thick cock shaft. A single sharp tug and Sabrina cried out, in pain as much as in ecstasy, spunk jetting from her cock even as the whip pulled away. Spurt after spurt came out as her body jerked in orgasm, soiling her balls and leaving her thick shaft decorated with long white streaks. She'd never once touched her cock, but for all that her fingers were locked into the arms of the chair. Adrienne gave a satisfied nod, well pleased with her handiwork, then turned to me.

'Lollipop time, Cochonette. Lick it all up, slowly.'

It was no more than I'd been expecting, and I was down on my knees in an instant and crawling over to where Sabrina waited, grinning. Adrienne moved a little to the side, trailing her whip down across my back and bottom as I got into position between Sabrina's thighs. My eyes were fixed on her cock and balls, thick with come that I had to lick up, and for a moment I just couldn't do it. Only when Adrienne's dog whip flicked against my naked bottom did I manage to shuffle forward and poke out my tongue to make a tentative dab at the mess on Sabrina's balls.

Another flick of the whip and I began to lick in earnest, running my tongue up the length of Sabrina's shaft to collect as much of her spunk as I could and showing Adrienne the dirty little pool on my tongue before I swallowed it down. I got another cut of the whip for my pains, and more stinging little flicks and carefully aimed lashes to warm my bottom as I began to clean up Sabrina's mess. I do like my mouth spunked in, and the feeling of knowing I've got a bellyful from my man when I go to sleep or on the way home, but this was different.

Both of them were watching and thoroughly enjoying my shame and the disgusted expressions I couldn't help making as I licked and kissed Sabrina's cock and balls. I could taste every drop, salty and musky at the same time, foul and yet utterly delicious, while I couldn't help showing off what was in my mouth over and over again. By the time I'd got her clean I'd abandoned my dignity completely and gulped her now half-stiff cock into my mouth, sucking eagerly and wishing that she was erect so that I could get another mouthful of what I'd been swallowing, maybe get fucked as well. I needed to come anyway, with my mouth full of the taste of shemale cock and spunk, but as I reached back to touch my cunt Adrienne gave me a harder cut of the dog whip.

'What do you think you're doing, Lucy? Did I say you could play with yourself?'

My answer was an incoherent gobbling noise as I still had Sabrina's cock as deep into my throat as it would go, but another cut of the dog whip made me pull back.

'I'm sorry ... I'm sorry, M'selle Adrienne, but I need to come.'

'I bet you do, you dirty little piglet, but this is a punishment, however much you're enjoying your disgusting behaviour. You come when I say you can come, not before.'

'Yes, M'selle Adrienne. Sorry, M'selle Adrienne.'

'That's better. Now give your hands to Sabrina and stick your bottom out. That's right, knees well apart, let's see those little pink holes.'

As I presented my bottom Sabrina took hold of my proffered wrists in a grip I knew I couldn't possibly break, leaving me trembling as Adrienne trailed the lash of her dog whip up over my cunt and between the cheeks of my bottom. It tickled dreadfully, and I began to squirm and giggle, completely helpless, only to cry out in pain as she snaked the whip around to deliver a hard cut full across the width of my cheeks. My bottom already felt hot and prickly, but she'd only been teasing before and I now felt as if I had a line of fire drawn across my rear cheeks. She chuckled to see my reaction. When she next spoke, her voice was cruel and yet calm, a tone I now knew hid her desire.

'Did you like the way I whipped Sabrina to orgasm, Lucy? Did you see her pain? I hope so, because now you're going to get the same. Hold her tight, Sabrina.'

The final order wasn't necessary. Sabrina had me trapped in a grip far too strong for me to break, while my face was against her still slippery cock, tempting me to lick and try to suck her as Adrienne continued to tease me with the whip. She'd got me to the point where I was wriggling my bottom for more before she gave me the next cut, which was harder still and drew a scream from my lips, and left me gasping for breath as she once more returned to tormenting me. I was squirming again as she snaked the lash up between my sex lips, my clitoris agonisingly sensitive to the plaited leather, and I quickly began to beg, only for my words to break into a fresh scream as the whip bit into my cheeks one more time.

Adrienne began to laugh, perhaps at the state she'd put me in, perhaps out of sheer cruelty, while Sabrina was wearing an impish grin. She started to get stiff again too, her cock growing as I rubbed my face against her crotch in abandoned pleasure, and as the whip settled between my bottom cheeks once more I took her back into my mouth and sucked eagerly as I was beaten. Adrienne gave a soft purr and began to tease my anus with the tip of her whip.

'What a dirty, dirty little pig you are, Lucy, sucking cock while you're whipped, and after everything that's been done to you. How many girls do you suppose could have their bottoms spanked in public, get taken home for a good rough fucking and still be happily sucking cock the next day? Not many, I'm sure. How many girls like to be spanked anyway? Quite a few, perhaps, but not like you, Lucy. And how many girls get off on being made to go down on complete strangers, Lucy? And how many girls get off on being put in a nappy?'

Sabrina laughed and I felt a powerful shudder of humiliation both at the exposure of my dirty secret and at Adrienne's betrayal. I'd thought it was our secret, something too intimate, too shameful to ever be admitted to anybody else, but she obviously didn't care, and had deliberately told Sabrina in order to add to my torment. It was too late, though, as all the while she'd been talking she'd been using the dog whip to tease my cunt and bottom hole, and I couldn't stop imagining how it would be, with me in my nappy and Sabrina watching as I was changed, rolled up, spanked, then put to her teat.

I was sobbing with shame as my head bobbed up and down on her now stiff cock, utterly lost to decency as the laughing Adrienne began to whip my cunt, laying the long strip of plaited leather neatly between my sex lips with every stroke, gently, but growing harder. Each and every cut caught my clitoris and I knew I was going to come immediately, powerless to resist either her or my own needs, with my bottom pushed well out and my knees spread wide. Both of them were laughing at me as I started to come, choking on cock as my muscles violently contracted and my head filled with obscene images: how I'd have looked spanked bare in the bar, or on the restaurant floor with my legs spread to show off my cunt, or having my nappy changed on my bed, or being whipped to orgasm as I sucked on Sabrina's cock.

The moment I was finished, Adrienne set on me, her poise lost to the demands of her own need. She'd twisted the whip in her hand and jammed it deep into my cunt while I was still in contraction, and she fucked me briefly before pulling it free and pressing it to my bottom hole instead. I tried to protest, weakly, but I was slippery with sweat and my own juices, and my ring spread before I could stop myself. With the whip well in up my bottom she grabbed me by the hair and pulled me around and between her thighs even as she settled on the sofa.

My head was pulled in, her stocking-clad thighs locking behind my neck to keep me in place as I began to lick her. She lay back so that I could attend to her anus as well as her cunt, and I did my best, lapping at her and burrowing my tongue in up both tight little holes, trying to concentrate on her pleasure but painfully aware of how I looked, with my bare bottom stuck up in the air and the whip protruding from my anus, my gaping cunt surely an invitation to Sabrina's now erect cock.

I got it, fucked from behind while she worked the whip in my bottom hole and I licked at Adrienne, both of them moaning and laughing in the joy of having me, utterly helpless and dishevelled, whipped to orgasm and made their little fuck toy, to be used exactly as they pleased until both had come, Adrienne in my face as I lapped at her clitoris, Sabrina deep up my cunt. They left me collapsed on the floor, exhausted, filthy, sore, but perfectly happy.

Chapter Six

It was just as well I was on the pill, or there would have been every chance that I was not only pregnant but in need of a DNA test to establish whether the father was a giant French butcher or a six-foot Brazilian shemale. Fortunately I've always been careful with myself and didn't have to worry, but I did need a rest. I thought that might mean another confrontation with Adrienne, but she simply remarked that it would be foolish to wear out such a pretty new toy and told me to go to bed early for the rest of the week. She also told me that she intended to hire me out at the weekend, which left me with butterflies in my stomach and in a state of ever rising apprehension as the days passed.

She wouldn't tell me the details, but I've always liked the idea of being hired out as if I were somebody's property, or a prostitute. It's a nice fantasy, and the more secure and successful I've grown, the more appealing it has become. I suppose that's because I've never really been at the risk of having to sell myself, since one call to my father would be enough to get me out of the most frightful situation.

So this was just right. I felt helpless, honour-bound to do as I was told by Adrienne, with no choice about who took me and what they did with me. Just the thought was enough to make me want to slip a hand between my thighs, and on the Friday evening, as I sat in my apartment after my bath, my fingers were trembling so badly that I was having trouble getting dressed.

I'd been told how to dress, as every girl who's made a plaything should be, and it was an exciting prospect. Somebody had been out shopping, somebody who knew my size and was happy to spend their money on me. Adrienne had laid it all out on the bed for when I got home: fully fashioned silk stockings, a pair of long black silk gloves, patent-leather heels from one of the best names in Paris, a little hat that looked as if it had come from a cabaret, and, best of all, a beautiful black corset embroidered with gold thread. There was also a Venetian mask in the same black and gold pattern as the corset and fringed with feathers, which suggested a masked ball.

If so, it was going to be the sort at which the women were expected to keep themselves sexually available, or at least very much on display. There were no panties, nor anything else to cover my bottom and pussy, while the corset was designed to display my breasts but without offering any concealment whatsoever. I'd be bare front and back, almost certainly in a large crowd, a plaything for my escort at the very least, and perhaps for many more.

As I rolled my stockings up my legs I was thinking of the opening of the *Story of O*, the best passage in the book in my opinion, and how similar my situation was, preparing myself in a Parisian boudoir while a taxi waited to take me to some unknown and thrilling destination. Not that I expected to be whipped bloody and thrown into the dungeon of some mysterious château, but it seemed reasonable to hope for an expensive townhouse and a good spanking.

Adrienne wouldn't tell me anything, and she wasn't coming, which added to my apprehension as she helped me into a long coat and walked me down to the taxi. There was somebody else in the back, and as I climbed in I saw that it was Marcelon, who greeted me with a knowing grin. In return, I gave him a brief flash of what was under my coat, eager to please but slightly surprised to find that he was my escort, and puzzled too. He wouldn't have been able to afford my outfit, for one thing, and it didn't seem his style either, but there he was – and no sooner had he given instructions to the driver than he pulled down his fly and freed his massive cock and balls. I swallowed involuntarily and cast a nervous glance towards the driver, who could hardly fail to see what was going on if I went down on Marcelon, as he clearly expected. Marcelon didn't care, but snapped his fingers in a preemptory fashion as he pointed to his cock.

'Suck me off. That's my payment for looking after you.'

I responded with a weak nod and gave the driver another worried glance as we drew away from the kerb. He seemed to be from North Africa, or perhaps the Middle East, and had a brown, weather-beaten face, a nasty little moustache and an even nastier and very large grin. I hesitated, wondering if I could strike some sort of deal with Marcelon, perhaps offering him a chance to spank me and fuck me again if I didn't have to suck him off in the back of the cab, but before I could decide what to say he lost patience with me and reached out one huge paw to take me firmly by the hair and draw me down into his lap.

My automatic protest was smothered as he rubbed my face against his cock and balls, but I held off for only a few seconds before allowing my mouth to open and take him in. The driver laughed at my inability to resist. So there I was, sucking cock in a French taxi as we drove across Paris. I was going to have to go all the way too, for Marcelon kept a tight grip on my hair as his cock began to swell in my mouth. He was obviously not prepared to put up with any nonsense.

He needn't have worried, because once I'd got him in my mouth the situation was too deliciously shameful for me to stop – though it was also wonderfully romantic, in a perverse sort of way. There I was, dressed like an upmarket call-girl, mouthing my escort's penis to pay him for looking after me, in the back of a public taxi with the coloured lights of the Parisian streets shifting across my body. We turned towards the city centre, crossing the Pont Mirabeau into crowded streets still heavy with evening traffic. Again and again walkers and other drivers had a chance to glimpse in at the taxi, and I was imagining their reactions to the sight of the pale oval of my face, half concealed by my mask, my mouth full of thick, virile cock and the man I was sucking holding me down by my hair.

Long before we'd reached our destination I was ready to be fucked, and the cab was full of the scent of expectant pussy. When Marcelon finally came in my mouth my strongest emotion was disappointment at the end of my ordeal. He made me swallow, holding me in place until I'd taken every last drop before I was finally released, to sit up and examine myself in my compact and make the necessary adjustments to my lipstick and eyeliner. I could see the driver in the mirror, his grin broader and dirtier than ever. Marcelon had casually put his cock away as if nothing had happened.

I had no idea where we were, nor did I really care, knowing only that I felt dirty and vulnerable, with my mouth full of the taste of Marcelon's spunk and my body nearly naked beneath my coat. Marcelon had undone my buttons so that he could grope my breasts as I sucked him, and I deliberately allowed the coat to fall open, which not only heightened my emotions but made the driver's grin expectant as well as dirty. I'd guessed I might be expected to suck him as well, to pay for the fare. Adrienne had clearly taken my liking for rough sex and lorry drivers to heart. Sure enough, as soon as we reached quiet roads beside an area of parkland, the order came. Marcelon asked the driver to pull over, then instructed me brusquely to get into the front and do my business.

The driver hadn't realised I was on the menu. He really was just the first person passing when Marcelon hailed a cab, so it was all the more humiliating for me to talk him into accepting a blowjob as payment for the journey. He made sure he got his money's worth, too. First he instructed me to get out on to the pavement, take my coat off and turn around to allow him to admire my body and my clothes, then he pulled me down onto his cock in the front of the car, while Marcelon watched as I sucked. I was groped, my breasts were explored and my nipples pulled, my pussy fingered and my bottom hole tickled, my cheeks squeezed and slapped … in fact, by the time he'd emptied the contents of his leathery brown ball sac into my mouth, I'd have happily let him fuck me. He didn't, but like Marcelon he made me swallow, and I was soon in the back of the car again, adjusting my make-up for the second time in quick succession.

We drove on. I was dizzy with need, my coat now fully open and my thighs wide, deliberately making an exhibition of myself. It was tempting to masturbate, showing the two of them exactly what they'd driven me to, but I held back, determined not to take the edge off my need when I knew I had a long night ahead of me. Also, I didn't know who I'd been given to, and I realised I might need my feelings of deep submission in order to cope, especially if it was some rich old man, as seemed likely. As it was I'd have accepted whatever they had in store for me – men, women, no matter how many, or of what age, or what they expected of me, my body was theirs for the taking, just so long as I got thoroughly used.

We had reached the very edge of the city before we stopped, in a district of expensive villas set in their own grounds, but the mansion at which we'd drawn up seemed to be some sort of clubhouse, and very patriotic, with crossed tricolors hanging over the front door and huge rosettes in red, white and blue decorating the balconies. Two massive, liveried doormen stood on either side of the entrance, but there was nobody else about, though the courtyard was crowded with cars, most of them large and expensive.

Marcelon came round to open the door for me, his manner now respectful and considerate, and offered an arm to escort me up the wide steps at the front of the building. The taxi left, the driver making a last rude joke at the expense of any man who kissed me, and I was ushered inside, into a great open room lit by huge, glittering chandeliers, its cloth-covered tables laden with dainties and bottles of champagne in ice buckets. I paused, trembling with nerves again as I realised that everybody present was old, at least the men; but my moment of panic, at the thought that I might be the sole entertainment for the evening, passed as I looked at the women. Every one was dressed in much the same style as I was, her breasts, her bottom and the triangle of fur or smooth pink skin between her thighs all bare, but set off with elegant lingerie and accessories, including masks and tiny, coquettish hats.

That was exactly what I'd been hoping for, but, as Marcelon slipped my coat from my shoulders to leave me in the same exposed state, my sense of panic came back, sharper than before. Most of the men were in uniform, and a sign on one side of the room announced a military reunion, which immediately set the alarm bells ringing in my head at the thought of running into M. Montesquieu. He might even be the one who'd hired me. I turned, intent on demanding the truth from Marcelon, only to see his grandfather approaching, in full Commandant's dress uniform, complete with a double row of medals. He was smiling expectantly and I felt a great sense of relief, realising that he was the one who'd hired me, although that didn't stop me taking a quick glance from side to side in case M. Montesquieu was there too. There was no sign of him, so I curtsied to Commandant Arnauld, lifting the lace edge of my corset as if it were a dress, which drew an appreciative nod.

'Very correct, my dear, and how very pretty you look. Champagne?'

There was a waiter nearby and I accepted a glass from his tray, swallowed it in one and immediately took a second. The Commandant ignored my poor manners and offered me his arm, leaving Marcelon by the door. I accepted, allowing him to steer me towards the buffet as he thanked me for coming and complimented me on my outfit, just as if I'd had any choice in the matter. There was an impressive spread of delicacies: foie gras, caviar, intricate hors d'oeuvres in a dozen styles, even ortolans, which I was fairly sure were illegal. Evidently this was no ordinary soldiers' reunion, but reserved for relatively well-off and dissipated officers, as no expense had been spared, the girls' outfits were hardly normal party wear and none of the uniforms showed the insignia of any rank lower than captain.

As I made a selection of delicacies the Commandant's hand moved to my bottom, first stroking my flesh, then kneading gently and finishing with a series of playful little pats, every one of which sent a sharp shiver through my body. It was what I was there for, after all, to be a decorative plaything, and he had every right to touch, but the implication that I might be spanked took things to a whole new level. I wondered what Adrienne had told him, certainly that I like my bottom smacked, but hopefully not how I'd reacted to being put in nappies, which was simply too much for the current situation. A spanking was another matter, especially as I was still high from my rough treatment in the taxi and no doubt deserved a punishment for giving in so easily. I pushed out my bottom, hoping Commandant Arnauld would get the message and put me across his knee then and there with the entire room watching, but he was busy inspecting the buffet even as he fondled my bottom and it was another man who spoke, from directly behind us.

'And a real blonde, even to her belly fur! Can there be another? Ah ha, I thought I recognised that perfect little bottom. It is Lucy, isn't it?'

I turned and stood transfixed, staring directly into the face of M. Montesquieu a few inches away, my mouth wide open, unable to move or speak but blushing furiously. It was no good pretending: my mask was unable to hide the fact that I was the tallest girl in the room and the only one with long, natural blonde hair. To add a final agonising touch of humiliation, he'd guessed it was me from the look of my cunt, also blonde, which he had seen – from the rear – when I slumped down on my bottom with no panties on in L'Alsacien.

He was more surprised than I was, and no wonder, to find his very English, very prim and proper senior assistant manager at what amounted to an orgy of degenerate old men and Parisienne tarts. Neither one of us knew what to say next, but Commandant Arnauld had no such difficulty.

'Ah, Claude, there you are,' he said, turning from the table. 'I see you know little Lucy already, or Cochonette as we must call her this evening. What a surprise! Claude was with me in Algeria,' he explained to me, 'right at the end, but quite the gamecock all the same.'

I finally managed to speak, desperate to rescue myself from the situation though it was obviously too late.

'Ah, yes, Claude and I work together, um ... Commandant Arnauld, um ... Pierre is a neighbour of mine, um ...'

My face felt so hot I must have been the colour of a beetroot, and I was stammering terribly, but M. Montesquieu had got over his initial shock, while Commandant Arnauld seemed indifferent to my embarrassment, carrying on as cheerfully as if we'd all met up in some fashionable café.

'Well then, as we're all friends together there's only one thing for it, a room upstairs and without delay! You fetch a couple of bottles of champagne and I'll call my grandson over. We shall have a little cabaret, not unlike the ones we used to arrange in the Bab el Oued, eh?'

M. Montesquieu gave a brief, admiring glance at my bare chest and nodded his head. 'Yes, why not, if Lucy's willing?'

Commandant Arnauld gave a soft chuckle.

'Oh, she's willing enough, I think. She's obliged to me, by her girlfriend, who likes to see her put to proper use. Once she's hot we can give her a Legionnaires' Triple, but her favourite thing is to be spanked, or so the girlfriend tells me.'

'Excellent, whoever's Tail End Charlie can spank her as he rides! Come along then, Lucy, or rather Cochonette, upstairs we go!'

He finished with a firm slap upon my bare bottom, not even troubling to ask if I was happy to submit to whatever indignity they had in mind for me. Even if he had, the answer would have been yes. Leaving my burning embarrassment and arousal aside, I realised, as they discussed what they were going to make me do, that the only sensible choice was to go along with them. As things stood, M. Montesquieu was merely a guest at a military reunion, albeit rather a peculiar one, while I had obviously allowed myself to be hired as a prostitute and I didn't even have the excuse of needing the money. Beyond even that, nearly all of my most personal secrets had been revealed within a few seconds: my bisexuality, my sexual submissiveness, my love of spanking.

Commandant Arnauld had gone to find Marcelon and it was M. Montesquieu who took me upstairs, collecting a couple of bottles of champagne on the way and responding cheerfully to the happy and envious remarks of his ex-comrades-in-arms, which kept me blushing hotly all the way to the second floor. The rooms had obviously been arranged in advance on the assumption that girls were likely to be taken upstairs, and keys were ready in the locks.

Some rooms were already in use, moans and sighs audible behind the doors. A waiter showed us to the fourth door along, asking if he could be of any assistance. He obviously hoped to fuck me, or maybe beat me or hold me down while the older men had me, for all I knew, and I would have complied, but M. Montesquieu declined his offer. I found myself in a richly furnished room with drapes of deep blue and a gigantic four-poster bed against one wall. I crawled onto it as he busied himself with the champagne, and as I did so Commandant Arnauld and Marcelon caught me with my rear view on full show. The younger man responded with an appreciative grunt, the older with a generous wave of his hand.

'She's all yours, my boy,' he said. 'Fuck her well and we'll join you presently. Oh, and put on a bit of a show, and don't rush it.'

Marcelon nodded. 'I won't, Grandpapa. I had her in the taxi already.'

With that he climbed onto the bed. I rolled over, eager to be just as dirty as they wanted, on my back with my legs spread and my cunt on offer, as Marcelon pulled off his shirt to reveal the sculpted muscles of his chest. He crawled up the bed, unzipped and offered his cock to my open mouth. I was sucking once more, and playing with myself at the same time, as the two old men settled down to watch.

I'd resigned myself to my fucking and whatever else they wanted to do to me, but the taste and feel of Marcelon's cock set me on fire. Not that he needed any encouragement, growing erect impressively quickly for a man who'd come not long before. I had my mouth fucked, first on my side and then with him squatting over my face as he drove his erection in and out while I fingered myself and teased at my clit in full view of our audience. Next I was mounted, but only for a moment, then I had his cock stuck back in my mouth to make me suck up my own juices before I was turned over and taken from behind, on my knees with his hard belly smacking against my bottom with every thrust.

By then both the older men had their cocks out and were pulling at their half-stiff shafts while they watched me being used. I wanted them both, and I didn't want any failures, so I waited until Marcelon gave me a chance to break free and I crawled to each of them in turn, to take them in my mouth and suck them hard. Both responded and then I was back on the bed, encouraged to ride Marcelon with my back to him as he slapped my bottom, then ordered to turn around as M. Montesquieu declared that it was time for the Legionnaires' Triple.

I had no idea what they meant, but I soon found out. I was on top of Marcelon, my cunt impaled on his glorious cock, my bottom thrust out and well spread to show off my bottom hole, already slippery with juice. To my mingled disgust and delight M. Montesquieu climbed up behind, pressed his erect cock between my cheeks and pushed himself in, deep up my bottom, grunting happily as he buggered me and pushing me down as I was presented with the Commandant's erection for my mouth. I took him in, sucking eagerly as the others pumped into me, now penetrated three ways with M. Montesquieu spanking my bottom as he buggered me.

They had me completely, their obedient little fuck toy, doing my best to please as I sucked and the two big cocks worked up my pussy and bottom hole, all the while with my bottom bouncing to my boss's slaps, used and abused, in a state of utter, wanton debauchery, but even that wasn't enough for them. No sooner had they got their rhythm up in me than M. Montesquieu called a change. Out came his cock, drawn fresh from my bottom hole and to my utter horror offered to my mouth even as Commandant Arnauld pulled me on top of him. I couldn't stop myself, my jaw instantly agape to take him in and suck, appalled by my own behaviour and yet lost in ecstasy. I knew what else was coming too, Marcelon's monstrous penis jammed in up my bottom hole until I felt I must split, but as the three of them began to thrust into me and the spanking began once more I knew I was going to come, and without even a touch of a finger to my clitoris. It was just too much, my complete degradation, at their hands but of my own choice, dressed up like a little tart, paying for my ride with my mouth, fucked and buggered and spanked, now with a cock in my mouth fresh from my bottom hole and another to come when they completed the triple by Marcelon making me suck him to orgasm as the others did theirs inside me.

Chapter Seven

No doubt plenty of women have woken up in bed with the boss, but not many in such exotic circumstances. I was stark naked except for my little hat and the long black gloves, and I could remember performing a striptease in front of a cheering crowd, standing on a piano while a man in tails played ragtime. That had presumably been after teaching them the rowing-boat game with five girls sitting on an enormously tall man with a beard like a hedge, because we'd been drinking champagne out of our shoes and I'd ended up barefoot. Then again I was sure the black girl who was now asleep on the far side of the snoring M. Montesquieu had been part of my team and I'd only met her when I'd been inviting people to lick custard off my tits, which had definitely been after my striptease.

One way or another, I had comprehensively disgraced myself, but then so had M. Montesquieu, behaving in a manner that would have had de Sade himself blushing, so that if there was one thing I could be absolutely certain of, it was that he was not going to be reporting me to head office. The memory of him feeding me the black girl's pussy juice off his erect cock once we'd gone up to bed was crystal clear, although I couldn't remember her name, which was a trifle awkward as I generally like to be introduced before doing that sort of thing, especially if one is likely to wake up in the same bed the next morning.

There were a lot of other things I couldn't remember either, such as what had happened to Commandant Arnauld and Marcelon. Both of them had come downstairs with me after giving me the Legionnaires' Triple, but at some point during the night I'd managed to lose them. That probably meant Adrienne was going to be cross with me, and another whipping, but she was going to have to wait. I was sore, my head hurt and the taste in my mouth was too awful even to think about. I had no idea how to get back to the Rue de la Cure anyway, although a good first step seemed to be to find some clothes.

I got out of bed, indifferent to my nudity as I went exploring, and found a towel in the passageway, too small to cover me properly but adequate as a skirt. The big hall downstairs was much as it had been when I went to bed, chaos, and I managed to find an outsize uniform jacket with four pips on the shoulder tabs and three rows of highly colourful medal ribbons. It came down far enough to cover my bottom, just about, and I abandoned the towel, which was unpleasantly damp.

A swallow of champagne and orange juice helped with the taste in my mouth and another of cognac restored a little energy. I collected some food from the remains of the buffet, went back upstairs and sat on the bed munching French bread spread with some exotic fruit paste and eating the occasional grape. It was half an hour before M. Montesquieu began to stir, and when he did he was clearly having as much trouble taking in the world as I'd had, blinking curiously first at me, then at the sleeping black girl, then back at me, only to shake his head as if in disbelief.

'M'selle Salisbury ... Lucy? What ... what are you doing here?'

'I was at the party, don't you remember?'

'Yes, but ... my God! And who is she?'

'I don't know. Would you like a grape?'

'Thank you, yes, but ... ah, yes, Pierre Arnauld and his grandson, we ...'

'I know, the Legionnaires' Triple, and that was just the beginning, but don't worry, I can keep a secret, and I'm sure you can too.'

'Yes, we had better, I think. What day is it, and why are you dressed as a Corps General? I thought you were more or less naked.'

'I was, and it's Saturday. I'll get you some orange juice. I think you need it.'

'I do, believe me.'

I went back downstairs, and by the time I returned he was sitting up in bed, and the black girl was awake too. Unlike me she'd managed to retain at least some clothing, but only a corset of brilliant green satin and one matching glove, which wasn't a great deal of use. She was called Nana, and to my relief she had a much clearer memory of the night before than we did, laughing over what we'd done and leaving no doubt at all about his behaviour.

She'd lost her escort, having been taken upstairs to suck him off quite early in the evening and then grown bored of his war reminiscences, so she'd asked to join in the boat race. I was blushing by then, thinking of what we'd done together. Not only had I sucked M. Montesquieu as he fucked her from behind, but I'd licked her bottom hole while he was up her pussy. Still, she took it all in her stride, laughing about the riotous bits and not mentioning the dirty ones.

Like me, she was stuck, without any money at all and with very little in the way of clothes, which left both of us reliant on M. Montesquieu. Fortunately he was a gentleman, and managed to get the staff to find my shoes and coat, while Nana took over the uniform jacket. Then he drove us back into the city and to his apartment in the 2nd arrondissement. I'd declined an offer of being dropped off in the Rue de La Cure, unable to face Adrienne until I'd at least had a shower, but I'd no sooner laid down on M. Montesquieu's ancient brass bed than I was asleep.

* * *

I woke from a dream in which a cartoon polar bear had got me by the leg, to find Nana shaking my foot. She was sitting on the end of the bed, still in the army jacket and holding out a steaming cup of coffee. I took it, sipped the hot black liquid and slowly regathered my senses. My first thought was a stab of self-recrimination for having broken what I'd intended to be an absolute rule: I'd allowed somebody at work to get involved with the more intimate side of my private life. Next I felt annoyed with Adrienne for not telling me the party was a military reunion, but then I remembered that I hadn't told her M. Montesquieu had been involved in the Algerian war, so it wasn't really her fault – it was mine, and I was going to deal with the consequences.

Those weren't the only consequences of the night before that I was going to have to deal with. I'd abandoned Commandant Arnauld and, although I couldn't remember what had happened, that wasn't going to stop Adrienne from taking it out on my bottom. She'd be waiting for me back at the Rue de la Cure, maybe genuinely worried, and I hadn't even sent her a text. That could easily be repaired, but eventually I was going to have to face her in person and take my punishment, although perhaps not until the following day. I nodded to myself, deciding to be firm with her, when Nana spoke.

'Do you think I might come home with you, Lucy?'

'Um ... perhaps. Haven't you got anywhere to go?'

'Yes, but I live in Beauvais and I've got no money, no keys, nothing. My flatmate won't be back until tomorrow evening.'

'Oh, all right then. What about the man you were escorting?'

'My bag was in his car, and my phone was in my bag. He didn't want me taking it in, because he said it spoilt my look.'

'Count yourself lucky. My girlfriend's probably going to spank me when I get home. Come on then, we'd better go, as I'm sure Claude needs his rest.'

She giggled at the idea of me being spanked, and after that there was never any doubt that we'd end up in bed. I'd enjoyed our play the night before, but it had mainly been for the benefit of M. Montesquieu, who'd wanted most of the attention on his cock. Now we had a chance to explore each other properly, and we'd no sooner reached my flat than we tumbled together on my bed, kissing and touching before going head to tail, her lovely dark bottom cheeks peeping out from under the uniform jacket, right in my face.

I had to do it – the velvety smooth, tightly puckered ring of her bottom hole was just too tempting – and I'd only been licking for a moment before I raised my head and pushed the tip of my tongue into the little black star. She sighed with pleasure, sat up and queened me in style, her bottom full in my face as I licked, only to give a sudden gasp and roll aside. At the same instant somebody spoke. The voice was all too familiar. Adrienne.

'Oh, hello, Lucy, hello, whatever your name is, and what exactly do you think you're doing?'

Even as my vision cleared I blushed and babbled half-hearted explanations, holding one hand over my boobs and the other between my legs, although in the circumstances it was a pretty pointless gesture. Adrienne was at the end of the bed, looking down at me, while Commandant Arnauld and Marcelon stood in the doorway. All three of them had seen it all before, but somehow that didn't make the situation any less embarrassing. I struggled to explain.

'... couldn't find you at all, and Claude had booked a room, so ...'

Adrienne took over. 'So you went to bed with him, and presumably with your little friend here?'

'Um ... yes. This is Nana.'

'Hello, Nana. Do you like to watch other girls being beaten?'

Nana shrugged, every bit as embarrassed as I was, with her jacket held closed at the front but still with the full length of her long black legs on show. Adrienne carried on.

'I do hope so, because that's what's about to happen. In fact, I'm not sure that your own tail couldn't do with warming. That's my girlfriend you're in bed with.'

Nana made a face, glanced at me, then back at Adrienne.

'Oh, sorry, but hey, we were just having a bit of fun. Anyhow, from what she tells me you're not so perfect yourself. You try me, you're going to be the one who gets her tail warmed.'

Adrienne's mouth fell open in outrage and for one awful moment I thought she was going to slap Nana's face, but at that instant Marcelon gave a low, dirty chuckle and passed a remark to his grandfather, something about how amusing it would be to watch a bitch fight. At that Adrienne swung around, her eyes blazing, but I stepped in quickly.

'There's no need for us to argue. Adrienne's right. I should have asked permission before playing with Nana, but we were really only carrying on from last night, when ...'

I trailed off, remembering that I'd been given to Commandant Arnauld, who hadn't had anything to do with Nana, but then rallied, hoping to bluff it out.

'Anyway, I probably do deserve a spanking, but can it wait until tomorrow, please, Adrienne? I'm tired, and –'

She cut me off with a curt laugh.

'Tired? It looked it, Lucy, with this piece of black tail sat on your face.'

It was Nana's turn to gasp in shock, and she came back right away.

'Look, I'm sorry I went with your girl, but one more crack like that and I'm going to give you what you give her, and a lot harder, so you just watch your mouth.'

'You little –'

'Ladies, please, be calm,' said Commandant Arnauld, stepping forward. 'I would hate to be the cause of any dissent between you, and doesn't it seem a shame to argue in what might otherwise be a rather promising situation?'

I hastened to back him up. 'Yes, let's not argue. I'm sorry, Adrienne, and you're welcome to spank me, right now if you want, but it's not Nana's fault, and you do play with whoever you like. I wasn't angry with Sabrina the other night, was I?'

Adrienne gave me a haughty look and made to reply, but Marcelon got in first, his deep voice rich with laughter and not a little lust.

'How about all three of you take a good spanking? Now that I'd like to see.'

Commandant Arnauld immediately nodded his agreement, and I saw that he'd taken a money clip of high-denomination Euro notes from his pocket, and was toying with then as if casually. Nana's gaze flicked to the notes and her expression softened as he spoke.

'I believe you were left out of pocket last night? Captain Lagrange left rather early, and not in the best of tempers, isn't that so?'

I'd never seen anything so blatant, but she didn't seem to mind, accepting several notes and tucking them into a pocket. For all the games I'd played, I'd never actually seen a girl bought before, and I felt a warm flush spread over my face and chest once more. I looked to Adrienne for support, suddenly painfully vulnerable, but she merely shrugged and I found myself wondering if she'd actually taken money from him for the night before, or, worse, if Commandant Arnauld had expected to pay me. My suspicions were immediately confirmed as he peeled off three more notes.

'You as well, naturally, my dear, even though we inadvertently became separated.'

'No, really, I …'

Adrienne reached out to take the notes, and for once she had the decency to show a little embarrassment as she answered him. 'Lucy doesn't take money, Pierre.'

I shook my head, struggling to find the words I needed, to explain that to me it was all just a game, but without offending Nana – whatever she might have done for money, what she'd done with me had been purely for pleasure. Then there was Adrienne, who had actually sold me, as the Commandant plainly had no idea we'd been playing a game, but then I'd gone along with it, and thoroughly enjoyed myself. He was plainly oblivious to my feelings, now beaming happily and rubbing his hands together as he carried on.

'Well then, girls, I think a spanking was mentioned? And I rather do think I owe you one, Lucy, you bad girl!'

'Um ...'

'Come along, young lady, Adrienne tells me you like it English fashion, so over my knee you go, and let's not have any nonsense!'

'Um ...'

Again I glanced to Adrienne for support, but all I got was a knowing little smirk and a wink before she spoke up in his favour.

'You did say you deserved to be punished, Lucy, and who better to do it than the Commandant, as he was the one you abandoned? So come on, over his knee you go. You can spank her with her own hairbrush, Pierre.'

She'd already picked the hairbrush up, and there was a wicked twinkle in his eye as he accepted it and beckoned to me.

'Come along, naughty little Lucy, time for a spanking.'

They all wanted me to get it, Adrienne, the Commandant, Marcelon, even Nana, who'd drawn back a little but was biting her lip in nervous excitement at what I was about to get. I gave in, resigning myself to fate as I swung my legs off the bed, despite the shame of being spanked in front of my new friend. They had me anyway: Adrienne and to some extent the Commandant were simply too good at pushing my buttons for me to resist, because I knew full well that if I didn't take what was coming to me I'd eventually regret it, but if I did it would be a memory to cherish among the best.

Defeated by my own treacherous needs, I quickly draped myself across the Commandant's legs, my bottom pushed well up. I didn't have any panties to pull down, so I was showing it all off from the start. Nana giggled to see me in such a humiliating position, while Marcelon stayed by the door, ensuring he got a good look at my rear as I was beaten. Adrienne seemed to prefer to watch the expression on my face. She sat down on the bed close to Nana and spoke to her as the hairbrush settled across my bottom.

'I am sorry I was angry, you weren't to know, but Lucy should have known better, and she certainly deserves to be spanked.'

It wasn't fair, and her words added a choking sensation of self-pity to my anguished feelings, but the next second the Commandant brought the hairbrush down across my bottom and everything was pushed from my mind but the pain of my spanking. A hairbrush hurts so much more than a hand, and despite his age he was strong and thorough, spanking me mercilessly hard, just as if he really did have a naughty girl across his lap. Maybe he actually saw it that way, and was intent on teaching me a good lesson. There was no doubt in my mind that I was being punished, the hard wooden hairbrush smacking down on my bottom again and again, harder and harder, leaving me writhing and kicking across his lap.

He wasn't about to stop any time soon, but spanked merrily away, and the state I was in only seemed to encourage him. Soon my hair was tossing wildly and my fists thumping on the ground in pathetic, futile remonstration, and all to the sound of my squeals, the meaty smacks of wood on tender bottom flesh and the cruel laughter of my audience. It was only when I lost my balance and fell off the Commandant's lap that it ended, with me sitting on my hot bottom and gasping out my feelings, while he began to clap.

'Quite a performance, my dear!'

Adrienne laughed.

'That was all real, Commandant. She's such a baby!'

I shook my head, still unable to find my voice, but very sure Adrienne would have made just as big a fuss in my place, probably more. Yet the spanking had done its magic. My bottom was warm and my pussy wetter than ever, definitely ready for a cock, as was my mouth. The bulge in Marcelon's trousers told its own story, and if the Commandant had unzipped I'd have been down on him in an instant, but he turned to Nana instead.

'And how about you? Don't you think you deserve it?'

She shook her head. 'Not like that you don't! It looked funny, but I don't think I could handle it.'

Adrienne gave a scoffing laugh. 'You could do better than big baby Lucy, surely?'

Nana was going to answer Adrienne back, but the Commandant had taken another pair of notes from his clip.

'A hundred Euros to see you spanked, Nana, by any one of us, by hand if you like, but it has to be for ten minutes by the clock.'

She made a face, pure contempt, then climbed off the bed and draped herself over his legs, exactly as I had been. He grinned like a satyr as he put his hand on her firm, dark cheeks, treating himself to a good feel, which she didn't seem to mind at all, and then started to spank. I got up, out of the way, but Adrienne immediately took me by the arm and pulled me down across her lap on the bed, face to face with Nana, so that I was looking right into her eyes as she struggled to cope with the pain.

There was sympathy in her face too, as my own spanking continued, and no doubt in mine too, because for all her bravado she wasn't doing much better than I had. He'd turned up her coat to get her bottom bare, and it was already wide open at the front, so her legs were kicking free and her heavy boobs bouncing as she began to give in to the stinging slaps he was raining down on her bottom. I took hold of her head and stroked her hair even as my own bottom was being given the same painful treatment, then kissed her, unable to resist, and in an instant our mouths were both open. Adrienne gave an angry hiss as she saw, and began to spank me harder still, but I was too hot behind and too turned on to care.

Ten minutes is an awfully long time to spank a girl, as anybody who's been given a really long session across the knee knows, but the Commandant was determined to get his money's worth and Nana determined to earn what she'd been promised. I could feel every slap as it ran through her body, and she was sobbing into my mouth as we kissed, but she wouldn't give in, even when he picked up the hairbrush and began to use that instead. Her jerks became harder, her sobbing more bitter, and as I opened my eyes I saw that she was crying, but still she stayed put, though her poor bottom must have been ablaze.

So was mine, hot and red behind me, but I was already broken to my own pleasure, eager for spanking and fucking and being made to lick Adrienne in front of them all, and anything else they wanted to do to me. I got it all, and more, the moment Nana's ten minutes were up. She was as far gone as me, and they put us on the bed, kneeling, our knees apart and our bottoms pushed up, black and white, side by side, both open and on offer. I got Marcelon's cock up my cunt, pushed deep in from behind while she was made to suck his grandfather erect and Adrienne stroked her blazing cheeks and teased the twin holes between. She let it happen, mouthing the Commandant's cock eagerly as she was masturbated, and she came before he was even properly hard.

That made no difference, for all that Adrienne was laughing to see Nana so turned on by her punishment. She stayed as she was, her bottom well lifted, allowing Marcelon to transfer his cock from my cunt to hers while Adrienne began to masturbate me in turn. It was what I needed, all my doubts and ill feelings dispelled as her fingers worked in my slit, tickling my bottom hole and teasing my clitoris, to bring me to ecstasy in just seconds.

I didn't stop, but pushed my face in beside Nana's to take a turn on the Commandant's cock while she licked his balls, her body rocking all the while to the firm, even thrusts of the monstrous cock inside her. A moment more and it was back inside me, Marcelon's huge hands tightly gripping my hips as the Commandant got into place behind Nana and eased himself in up her hole. We were kissing as we were fucked, our mouths open together in ecstasy as their bellies slapped on our hot bottoms and their cocks pumped in our cunts, two spanked girls side by side, punished and fucked and finally spunked in, just as it should be.

Chapter Eight

With my introduction to Nana I had well and truly given myself over to the darker side of Paris. I wasn't sure exactly what Adrienne got up to, and even Sabrina played mainly for kicks, but Nana was a call-girl. When it came to sex for its own sake she preferred other girls, and she earned her living, if not exactly on the streets of Paris, then by escorting men to Parisian events, and taking her to bed afterwards was very much part of the deal.

For all my guilt and shame and self-recrimination for risking my position at work, I found the whole thing intensely thrilling. When I arrived at work on Monday morning to find among my correspondence an envelope containing two hundred Euros, I nearly came then and there. There was no explanation, only a business card marked with a single cursive M, but I knew full well who it was from: M. Montesquieu. He'd bought me, paid for the use of my cunt just as he had for Nana.

I knew I should have given the money back and explained the situation to him, but it was far more exciting to accept it, and have him know I'd accepted it, although I wasn't sure if he was simply playing a game or genuinely thought I expected money for my services. Either way it was exhilarating, and opened up some intriguing possibilities, but I didn't want to talk about it, which would only spoil the thrill. I did want more, and most of all, best of all, I wanted to be put across his knee and spanked.

He could pay me or he could punish me, but what I really wanted was for him to pay Adrienne, who would then send me to him for a punishment. I knew she'd do it too, and the prospect was so exciting I couldn't stop thinking about it. In the end I had to make a trip to the female executive washroom, where I sat down in a cubicle with my panties pulled aside, my head full of shame and swimming with dirty images as I masturbated.

I was no sooner back at my desk than an email arrived from Magnus to say that he was going down to the Charentes to buy cognac and asking if I'd like to come. Despite all the fun I'd been having I felt instantly home-sick and badly in need of his big, comforting arms, preferably for a long loving cuddle while I confessed my sins before being turned over his knee, spanked until I howled, then fucked. Unfortunately there was no way for me to justify taking the second half of the week off, especially when I was on a drive to make everybody else work their proper hours.

The best I could do was to take a TGV south after work on the Friday, which would allow me to reach Angoulême, where Magnus could pick me up in time for dinner. I could return on the Sunday afternoon, giving me two nights in his company, a thought that set my tummy fluttering and very nearly sent me back to the loo. He quickly agreed to the arrangement, and I was left with a delicious sense of anticipation, making it all the harder to force myself to concentrate on my work.

Adrienne had still been asleep when I left the apartment, as I'd had to get up early to get Nana on her way to the train before going into work. I'd decided it was best to tell her about Magnus face to face, and was feeling a little apprehensive as I climbed the stairs of her building. She was sure to punish me, that was part of the deal, and for all my fear of the pain it was very much a positive thing, but despite our agreement it was obvious that she would prefer to have me fully under her control. I was going to have to be firm.

I caught the scent of cooking as I opened the door, and found her in the kitchen cutting bread, a pot bubbling on the stove. She was in old jeans and a baggy top, with an apron on, very casual for her, so I clearly wasn't in for an impromptu thrashing. I kissed her and took a sniff at the pot.

'That smells good. What is it?'

'Just some veal, red wine, shallots, anything to hand really.'

'Yum, I'm starving. Thank you for everything over the weekend, that was really special.'

'I thought you'd enjoy it, you little tart.'

'For you, always. Um … next weekend I'm seeing Magnus, by the way.'

'Your Viking? Good. I'll invite Marcelon over and they can take turns with you, or maybe have you together on a spit roast.'

'Yes, please, but that will have to be another time. He's in the Charentes, so I'm going down to Angoulême by train and coming back on the Sunday night.'

'Oh.'

She sounded disappointed and I immediately felt horribly guilty and hung my head. 'I'm sorry, Adrienne. I'll make it up to you, I promise.'

I was trying to think of an offer I could make, something to inspire her sadistic nature, but she'd gone back to cutting the bread, now with pointed vigour, but she didn't speak. It was hard to know what to say, beyond apologies, but I was determined to make her accept my decision, and to acknowledge me. I got down on my knees and looked up at her with my hands under my chin as if I were a puppy begging for the approval of her mistress.

Adrienne tried to ignore me, but I could see the corner of her mouth twitching as she struggled not to smile. I nuzzled my face against her leg, kissing the material of her jeans with my eyes raised to hers as I moved gradually around to her bottom. She cuffed me gently on the side of my head, but when I didn't stop she drew a patient sigh and pushed out her bottom.

'Go on then, Cochonette, if you must, and I suppose I'll let you have your Viking, if you're very, very good all week.'

'I promise.'

I'd got behind her, my face pushed against her bottom as my fingers found the button of her jeans. She'd made her point, giving me permission rather than accepting my choice, and I assumed that all would be well. Keen to do my best to please her and to show both my submission and my gratitude, I quickly had her jeans and panties down at the back and my face pressed well in between the cheeks of her bottom. She gave a little sigh as my lips found her anus and kissed the tight little star in what must surely be the most devoted gesture of submission a lover can give. With that she rested her elbows on the worktop and pushed out her bottom to let me get at her properly.

My tongue was already well in up her bottom hole and I spared myself nothing, licking as deep as I could get, to leave her slit wet and clean before I pushed in

117

deeper to get to her cunt. I could barely breathe or see, my face completely smothered between her beautifully rounded little bottom cheeks and my tongue busy with her clitoris, but now I was doing it as much for myself as for her. My skirt came up and my hand slipped inside my panties to rub at myself as I attended to her pussy and her bottom hole, turn and turn about, as our excitement rose together. I made her come first, which was only right, with my face pressed deep between her cheeks as I licked her to ecstasy. Then I turned my attention to my own needs, my fingers snatching at my own urgent cunt and my tongue thrust up her bottom hole as far as it would go.

* * *

Now that I'd cleared everything up with Adrienne I was able to enjoy a sense of rising anticipation each day for the second week in a row, although this time she made sure to use me well. I was punished every evening, either spanked across the knee or taken to task with her dog whip, after which she'd either sit on my face or lie back so that she could sip a glass of wine as I knelt to lick her. On the Wednesday I got my spanking in front of Commandant Arnauld, whom she'd called round purely to add to my humiliation, and was made to suck his cock as well, for which he paid five euros. On Thursday it was Sabrina, and a double spanking over their joint laps before having to thank them both with oral sex. All of it was good, but it did nothing to reduce how much I was looking forward to seeing Magnus – just the opposite, in fact.

On the Friday morning the time seemed to crawl, despite my busy schedule. M. Montesquieu had arranged a management conference for 5 p.m. and I knew I would have to stay to the last minute. During the conference I forced myself to play my part as I should, but to my irritation he asked to speak to me once the others had gone. His manner had been completely professional, even rather cool considering what had happened between us, and to my surprise he continued in the same way once the last of our colleagues had left the office.

'There is a rather important matter to discuss, Miss Salisbury. No, don't sit down.'

I closed the door. I was surprised by his attitude, and his tone, which was more what I'd have expected a rather insecure boss to use to the officer junior than how he should have been addressing me.

'Is there a problem, Monsieur Montesquieu?'

He didn't reply for a moment, tapping a pencil on the desk and watching me from beneath heavy eyebrows. Everybody else was on their way home, and he didn't speak until he'd heard the distinctive thud of the main security door.

'Yes, Miss Salisbury, there is a problem. Your attendance has been poor, your work has been unsatisfactory and your dress has been frankly slovenly.'

For an instant I wondered what he was talking about, and was about to answer with genuine pique when I caught on. I stifled a laugh and replied. 'Yes, sir. Sorry, sir.'

He drew in his breath and steepled his fingers.

'Furthermore, I learn from your friend Adrienne Vauligneau that you have been attending the sort of party that risks bringing the company into disrepute. Therefore I regret to say that "sorry" is simply not good enough. In fact, Miss Salisbury, I am very much afraid that I have no alternative but to put you across my knee and spank your bare bottom.'

I'd guessed what was going on, and he was really hamming it up, but he was still my boss and he was still threatening me with a spanking, an opportunity too good to miss. A glance at my watch showed that I had time, as long as I got on with it, but I had to make a bit of a fuss.

'No, sir, not that! Please don't spank me! I'm ... I'm too old to be spanked, especially bare bottom. It's not proper!'

'Nonsense! You're not too old at all, not when I'm the one doing the spanking, young lady, and besides, going bare bottom will do you the world of good. Now get over my knee, Miss Salisbury, let's not have any nonsense.'

'No, please, I'm begging you!'

He shook his head and pushed his chair back from the desk, making a lap for me. I'd imagined the situation a thousand times, when a man with real authority over me would order me to get over his knee so that he could pull down my panties and spank my bare bottom, and his next words were like an electric shock.

'I'm in charge here, young lady, and I'll decide what's good for you, when you need spanking and when your panties have to come down, so over you go, right now.'

Either Adrienne had been coaching him on how to treat me or he'd been visiting British spanking websites, for he had chosen his words to leave me incapable of resistance. I stepped forward to drape myself across his legs. It felt so nice, across my boss's lap with my bottom lifted for spanking, and as he fumbled up my skirt and slip I was in a state of bliss, my mouth wide and my eyes closed, every word he spoke sending a jolt of shame-filled pleasure through me.

'Yes, Miss Salisbury, I know you're a fully grown woman and this may be rather embarrassing, but that's rather the point, isn't it? So up comes your skirt, and down come your panties.'

He eased my knickers down and I was bare bottom, across my boss's knee, in his office, about to be spanked. It was pure ecstasy, but he wasn't finished with me.

'Yes, panties down, if only to remind you that a

121

naughty girl loses her right to modesty. If you didn't want to end up with your privates on show, well, you should have thought about that earlier, shouldn't you?'

All I could manage in reply was a choking sob, and then he held me around the waist and began to spank me. With the very first smack I knew I was going to come. He'd delivered it right to my sweet spot, at just the right strength, sending a shock of ecstasy straight to my pussy. The situation he'd put me in was perfect. As the smacks went on I was running it over in my head again and again, how I'd been made to go across my boss's knee, told off as my skirt was turned up and my panties taken down, then spanked.

He'd only given me thirty or forty smacks when my orgasm hit me, welling up in my head to burst in an explosion of ecstasy, my bottom pushed up to his hand and my thighs as wide apart as my knickers would permit. I must have looked a sight, with my cheeks squeezing and my bumhole winking between, my cunt wet and juicy and my entire body shaking, and it certainly got to him. A moment later I was tumbled off his lap, his fly was wrenched open and his cock stuffed into my mouth.

I sucked with all the gratitude of a girl who's just been spanked to orgasm, using every trick I knew to please him as I worked on his cock. When he finally spunked in my mouth, I made sure that I swallowed every drop. With that done, I had to go. It had been sweet of Adrienne to set me up, and though her timing seemed less than perfect I could see the virtue in sending me off on my weekend with a hot bottom, as it was just the sort of cruel, rude behaviour I enjoy the most.

My TGV was leaving from the Gare Montparnasse in less than an hour, but I'd got everything packed and ready, and simply slung my bag over my shoulder and threw myself into a cab directly opposite the office doors. It was only as I collapsed into the seat that I realised my mistake, as the cab was already occupied, but before I could apologise and retreat my fellow passenger had grabbed me, pulled me forward and pressed a greasy rag against my mouth, even as he slammed the door.

I struggled, desperate to break free as the cab jolted into motion, but my captor was big, male and far too strong for me. He also smelt of fresh meat, the rag he'd forced into my mouth tasted of blood as well as grease, and he was calling me Cochonette as well as a bitch and a slut as he used my jacket to trap my arms into the small of my back. I'd been kidnapped by friends of Marcelon, undoubtedly to be taken somewhere quiet and thoroughly used, which would have been just fine except that I needed to be at the station.

He either thought I hadn't realised what was really going on and assumed my ever more desperate struggles were real panic and fear, which made him a genuine, twenty-four carat bastard, or he liked to play hard, because he was slapping my face to try and calm me down while he made a thorough job of taping the greasy rag into my mouth and securing my hands behind my back. With that I was completely helpless, but still kicking until he managed to get my panties down my legs and tie them off at my ankles before adding more tape.

I was still trying to make him realise he'd got it wrong, but he either thought I was acting or just didn't care, and enjoyed a leisurely grope of my bottom and boobs as we drove through the evening traffic. He swapped jokes with the driver about how wet I was as he eased two massive fingers into my cunt. He was right. I was soaking, maybe partly because of the way they'd caught me and manhandled me, but mainly because I'd been spanked to orgasm after spending most of the day thinking about what I was going to get that evening.

But now I wasn't – or rather I was, but not in the way I'd anticipated. My only chance seemed to be that they'd want to make me suck cock before fucking me, and then I'd be able to explain the situation. I was scared too, because it was at least possible that they'd planned this on their own. Obviously Adrienne didn't know about it, or she wouldn't have let them kidnap me when I was supposed to be going to the station. That thought made me wriggle all the harder, and earned me another slap. Then, as the taxi slowed to a stop, Marcelon himself climbed in. He laughed at the state I was in, bound and gagged with my skirt rucked up and my panties pulled down to show off my pussy.

I made eye contact, trying to make him realise I was in real trouble, but he just grinned at me and promptly made my situation worse by ripping my blouse open and tugging up my bra to bare my boobs. He began to grope me as the cab started off once more, and his friend's fingers soon slid up my cunt again. Still I wriggled, but it only seemed to encourage them and they could hold me down with no real difficulty. By the time we finally stopped I was in a desperate state, my clothes ruined, my cunt soaking. They both had their cocks out, Marcelon rubbing his in my hair and over my face while his friend got his jollies against what was left of my stockings and on my bare thighs.

We were in some back alley lined with garages, maybe near Marcelon's house, maybe not. I was dragged out of the cab and into one of the garages and thrown down on a filthy mattress. The door closed behind us and I was squirming in my bonds as the three of them looked down at me, grinning, their erect cocks sticking up out of their flies, ready to have their fun with me. I did want it, and at any other time it would have been a wonderful treat, so long as I knew I was ultimately safe, but when Marcelon jerked the tape from my face to ready my mouth for cocksucking I spat out the rag and immediately began babbling.

'No, not now! Stop it, you idiots, I'm –'

My words broke into a wet gulping noise as Marcelon's erection was jammed down my throat, so I had enough trouble trying to breathe, never mind speak. He climbed on top of me, fucking down into my mouth as his friends took hold of my legs and rolled me up to expose my cunt. I got fucked, and I didn't even know who went first, either the big man who'd subdued me in the taxi or the driver, simply mounting me and stuffing his cock up my hole without further ceremony.

That was only the start. All three of them were determined to make full use of me, which seemed to mean for as long as possible and in every hole. Even before the taxi driver decided to stick his cock up my bottom I was too far gone to really care, and so slippery it went right up with a couple of good shoves. By then I was helping, still tied up in my ruined clothes but sucking eagerly on their cocks and showing off my bottom and cunt for entry. They weren't going to stop anyway, not until all three had come, and the best thing I could do was to help them get there as fast as possible and pray that if I made all three happy they'd help me to catch a later train.

Marcelon was the first to come, deep up my cunt, while I sucked the driver's cock and the one I could only think of as my kidnapper buggered me. That left two, and the driver, who had already put it up my pussy and my bottom hole, was now holding me by my hair as he fucked my throat. He'd soon emptied his balls, leaving the last man, the kidnapper, who made a point of easing his cock in and out of me nice and slowly, one hole after another, before giving me the final degradation by using his helmet to rub me off then jamming himself up me one last time to cream in my aching, sopping cunt.

The instant he was done they were laughing, making a joke of how they'd used me and my pathetic, helpless reaction. Marcelon undid the tape around my wrists and ankles, none too gently, while the driver fetched me a cold beer from a fridge in one corner. I couldn't even speak clearly until I'd taken a couple of mouthfuls, and even then my ability to talk in French seemed to have deserted me, but I finally managed to make myself clear to Marcelon.

'No, it was fine ... thanks, but it shouldn't have been tonight. I'm supposed to be on a train to Angoulême. What time is it anyway?'

'Half past six.'

'That early? We can make it, maybe. How far to the Gare Montparnasse from here?'

'Twenty minutes, maybe half an hour.'

'Can we go, please, quickly? Never mind what happened, let's just go!'

They were doubtful, exchanging worried looks and sharp bursts of conversation, asking me again and again if I was really OK, but for all the doubts and misgivings in my mind I was determined to make the train. My bra was ripped and my panties beyond saving, my blouse torn and my stockings in tatters, but my skirt and jacket were intact and by the time we got to the Gare Montparnasse I was merely dishevelled. There was no time to fuss anyway, for my train was already preparing to leave as I raced across the concourse and through the barrier. The doors were closed and a guard was signalling to the driver in the rear engine, who had his door fractionally open as the great train started to move. I caught the handle, jerked it wide, threw myself in and collapsed on the floor, panting for breath as the astonished driver looked down at me, his eyes fixed on the bare pink tit peeping out from my open blouse.

'You're a pretty one.'

Chapter Nine

The spare driver on a TGV doesn't have a lot to do, except amuse himself with any random girls who happen to jump into his cab at the last second. That was what the one on the Paris–Bordeaux TGV did with me anyway, first making me get down on my knees to suck his big fleshy cock to erection then fucking me over the instrument panel while the French countryside faded out behind us at 200 miles per hour.

From the instant I read the implications of the dirty grin on his face I had resigned myself to another fucking. I was perfectly ready and, besides, I was getting used to being treated that way. It was the sensible thing to do, anyway, because if there's one thing I've learnt about men over the years it's that if they've had their fun and think you might be up for more they'll be as helpful as can be. Mine certainly was, chatting happily and not even demanding another suck until we were past Niort.

That left me plenty of time to reflect on the situation,

and the more I thought about it the more convinced I became that Adrienne had deliberately tried to stop me going south for my weekend with Magnus. Having me spanked by M. Montesquieu was suspicious, but she knew I wanted to be dealt with by him, and she also knew all the little things I enjoy that make a punishment as deliciously humiliating as possible. She'd obviously given him exact instructions, and must have known what it would do to me: either send me on my way to Angoulême with a hot bottom and a wet pussy, or maybe make me change my mind and spend the night with him.

Yet she knew me better than that. I love to be sexually humiliated, and I can get pretty carried away when I'm turned on, but I am organised and I am efficient. I keep my appointments, even if I get spanked pink and rogered senseless on the way. It was the rogering that was harder to explain ... after all, Marcelon and his friends had actually got me to the station on time, and, looking back, they'd been remarkably quick. It's hard to keep track of time when three big men are using you as a fuck toy, but I couldn't possibly have been in the garage for more than half an hour.

I wanted the whole thing to be a carefully orchestrated plan to put me on the train in a state of high excitement and deep shame, but I couldn't shrug off the possibility that Adrienne had set it all up to keep me away from Magnus. If the latter, then she'd failed, but if the former she had succeeded in spectacular style. I did my best to tidy myself up, but when I got off the train at Angoulême I had no panties or bra, I'd abandoned my torn stockings and my blouse was held together with a piece of string the driver had found in his pocket. My hair and make-up were OK, as I still had my bag, but I wasn't in an ideal state to greet my boyfriend, or my girlfriend.

Magnus always stuck out from the crowd, his massive frame and ginger hair setting him apart in any situation, let alone among the passengers on a fairly rural French railway station, and with him was Stacey. Just to see them made my chest ache with longing and homesickness, and I'd no sooner kissed them than I was pouring my heart out, going back over most of what they already knew and explaining everything they didn't, from my adventures in French long-haul lorries to the moment the train driver had come in my mouth just a few minutes earlier. They took it all in, by turns amused, supportive and aroused. When I was done Stacey summed it all up in one sentence.

'You deserve every punishment you get, Lucy, and more, but you are all right, aren't you?'

Just to hear the sympathy in her voice brought me to the edge of tears, but my answer was genuine.

'Yes. It's been great, tough at times, but great. I could wish Adrienne was a little more supportive, but she has given me some experiences I'll never forget. I suppose

Lucy Salisbury

she felt she had to push my boundaries to really get me there, and it's true, but I could have done with a few more cuddles, perhaps.'

'Poor Lucy.'

Magnus was driving and Stacey and I were in the back. She took me in her arms, hugged me and stroked my hair. Her breasts were pressed against me, full and proud, kindling a sudden, desperate need to be suckled by her, something she'd often done to soothe my feelings. She didn't need telling but unbuttoned her blouse and lifted one heavy globe free of her bra to feed her nipple into my mouth, suckling me as I clung on with the tears streaming down my face. Magnus spoke from the front.

'Are you all right back there?'

Stacey adjusted her grip before she answered, cradling me in her arms.

'It's OK, she just needs to let her feelings out a little so I'm giving her a feed.'

Magnus understood and didn't reply, although from his reaction when we'd done it in front of him I knew the blood would be pumping to his cock. I'd be the one to deal with that, in due course, but for the moment I was content to suck on Stacey's nipple as she stroked my hair and petted me gently, all my ill feelings slipping rapidly away as we drove through the gathering darkness.

Their hotel was in Cognac, not all that far away and along a fast, straight road. As Stacey suckled me I was growing ever more desperate for full sex, and with Magnus involved. I'd have happily done it in a convenient aire, just as I had for Jean-Paul what seemed an age ago, but Magnus increased his speed and we were soon in town. The moment we were safely in their room I stripped off, fully naked, to go down on Magnus's lovely pale cock for a few minutes before making for the shower. When I came out Stacey was topless and Magnus sat next to her on the bed, his cock and balls out as she nursed his erection.

They didn't need instructions, but handled me with an expertise born of long practice. I was put across Stacey's lap to be spanked and teased from behind while I sucked Magnus's cock, revelling in his size and the taste of him until he gave me what I needed so badly and came in my mouth. Stacey came next, her jeans and panties pushed down and her thighs spread to me as I licked her to ecstasy, with my bare red bottom pushed out behind so that she could see what she'd done to me. And then it was finally my turn.

I got it lying across Magnus's lap, with my bottom pushed up for spanking as he punished and masturbated me at the same time, while my upper body was cradled in Stacey's arms as she fed me at the teat and stroked my hair. When my orgasm came it went far beyond simple sexual pleasure, a moment of sublime ecstasy that left me not just content and satisfied but completely fulfilled.

* * *

When I'd come upstairs I'd noticed that they'd booked a single room with two double beds, and that night Stacey and I shared one while Magnus took the other. It was a purely practical choice, given his bulk, and in any case I was too tired and sore to do more than collapse, but in the morning I found myself wondering what had been going on in London since I'd left. Magnus and Stacey weren't exactly compatible, but they did have a lot in common in that both liked submissive girls. They seemed a lot closer than they had been when I'd said goodbye a few short weeks before. I had to ask, and tackled Stacey over breakfast while Magnus was still upstairs.

'Are you two together now?'

She went ever so slightly pink and I was forced to bite down a sudden pang of jealousy.

'Um ... sort of. We can talk together, that's the thing, and I suppose we're both in love with you, but you're not there, and ...'

She trailed off, still looking embarrassed, although she had no reason to be. They'd shared me twice before I left, and on the second occasion Magnus had fucked Stacey while she and I were in a sixty-nine, so all they'd really done was carry on where we'd left off, but without me. I hastened to reassure her.

'That's OK. I understand, as long as I'm not excluded.'

'Of course not, don't be silly, and when we come to

Paris I hope we're not going to be excluded either. To be honest, your new girlfriend sounds a bit of a bitch.'

'She is, that's why she's so good, but she never really turns it off, and she is a complete control freak. Don't worry, though, I've struck a deal with her, that I can play with you and Magnus as long as she can do exactly as she pleases with me while I'm in Paris.'

'I bet you love that. What a perfect excuse to let her be really mean with you. You're terrible, Lucy!'

'That's true, and it was great when she sold me to Commandant Arnauld for the night, but I'm worried she'll take it too far. As I was saying last night, my boss knows what I'm into now, although that wasn't her fault, but now she's having him spank me, and again it's just what I want, but it's risky. The last night, with the three men – I can't work out if she set it all up very carefully just to play with my feelings or if she wanted to mess up the weekend for me to keep me away from Magnus.'

'I couldn't begin to guess, but you're going to have to speak to her.'

'It's not easy. She doesn't necessarily say what she thinks. She loves to play mind games with me, and she genuinely believes that it's for the best if she makes the decisions. Maybe it is, as far as getting me off is concerned, but it's not safe. Anything might have happened last night, either when Monsieur Montesquieu was spanking me or during the kidnapping. You're right, though, it's going to have to be done, but I refuse to let that spoil my weekend. Last night you mentioned the beach?'

'Yes, if Magnus can be persuaded to drive that far. It's quite a way, apparently, but he says there are places you can walk for miles without seeing anybody, it's so lonely.'

It was, a stretch of pale sand between land and sea, far from easy to get to and completely deserted, although not completely unobserved, because when we arrived several boats were visible a little way out to sea. They were gathering mussels, or perhaps oysters – hardy French fishermen, which made it all the more enjoyable to strip naked, knowing they could see us but only as distant figures. Stacey was little shy at first, but soon abandoned her swimming costume to join me, and we ran naked along the sand and played in the surf together while Magnus watched us and sipped a cold beer.

As always when I manage to get away from my normal life, I was soon wishing I could give up my job and everything that went with it, to live a carefree, idle existence, spending most of my time casually naked. I knew it wouldn't work, that I'd be bored in moments, but for the time being I was delighted to be able to enjoy the freedom and solitude, so very different after Paris, where I'd never really been alone for a moment and there was the constant background noise of the city.

When I needed to pee I simply squatted down and

let it all go, gushing from my pussy in a long, glittering spray to splash onto the wet sand. Stacey was right next to me and put on a shocked face but made sure to watch. So did Magnus, and the moment I was done he beckoned to me to come to him. I knew what was going to happen and I didn't mind in the least, happily running up the warm sand to drape myself naked across his legs without having to be told.

He spanked me, nude, in full view of the distant fishing boats, and it was so quiet that their crews must have been able to hear the fleshy smacks and my squeals of shock and pain. Stacey watched the entire performance with her arms folded across her chest, wearing an expression of amused superiority that turned me on almost as much as the spanking. When he was done with me Magnus announced that as part of my punishment I'd have to stay naked until we left.

I hadn't planned to get dressed anyway, but now I'd been told to go naked, which made it sexual. I've always loved running around with no clothes and a hot red bottom, which brings back so many happy memories. My excitement was infectious and, although Magnus seemed content to watch and wait, my games with Stacey quickly grew more intimate. She found a huge seaweed stalk, just like a whip, and chased me with it, far along the beach, until I gave in and collapsed to my knees with my bottom lifted in surrender.

A couple of hard strokes brought me even further

on heat and as she threw the seaweed aside I rolled on my back and opened my arms to her. She was about to mount me but glanced out to sea, where the fishing boats were still visible but a lot further away, then looked up towards the long lines of dunes that lay between us and the land beyond.

'Hang on,' she said. 'I need to pee.'

I knew exactly what I wanted on the instant.

'Do it all over me.'

'Lucy, you dirty girl!'

'Why not? I can go in the sea afterwards, and it would be so nice. Come on, Stacey. You can even do it in my mouth if you like.'

'Lucy!'

'Please, Stacey.'

She gave another doubtful glance towards the fishing boats, but they were much too far away to see what was going on, at least in any detail, while I was so turned on I rather liked the idea of being watched anyway. They'd already seen me spanked, and now they could watch me pissed on, and more, if Stacey decided to deal with me properly. She nodded and I knew it was going to happen. I spread myself out on the sand, naked and vulnerable, my mouth open, and Stacey straddled me, her feet planted on either side of my waist and her belly pushed out.

'OK, you dirty little bitch, if this is what you really want?'

'Yes, please, all over my tummy and tits, and in my mouth, you have to do it in my mouth.'

'You're a disgrace, Lucy.'

She'd already spread her pussy, and as she spoke she let go, aiming a strong pale-gold stream between my breasts. I closed my eyes and let it happen, delighting in every second as she peed all over me, loving both the warm, wet feeling as I rubbed it over my breasts and belly and the exquisite humiliation of having another woman urinate on me. When she went lower I spread my thighs as wide as they'd go, teasing my cunt as the hot piddle splashed in my slit and between the cheeks of my bottom, over my belly and down my legs.

I began to masturbate as she moved higher once more, my jaw wide to receive what she had to give me: hot golden fluid, full of the taste of girl, splashing in my face and filling my mouth to trickle out around my lips. As she finished she squatted down, to let the last trickle of pee fall on my face before pressing her cunt to my mouth. I swallowed what I'd already taken in, a deep gesture of submission to the girl whose pussy I'd begun to lick as I rubbed at my straining clitoris.

A moment more and she'd swivelled around to put her bottom in my face the way I like it, smothering me between her big, firm cheeks and allowing me to lick at the tight little hole between before returning my attention to her cunt. I was going to come, and as I masturbated with ever more urgency I was imagining what the fishermen could see, and hoping they had binoculars. My cunt was spread open to them and to Magnus, my body wet with piss from the girl who was now sitting on my face, bare bottom, my fingers busy in my slit, masturbating because I'd been pissed on. We came at the same moment, in a wonderful mutual orgasm that left us collapsed together on the sand, kissing and laughing as the surf washed over us.

I knew I was in trouble, because while Magnus was a long way away he had undoubtedly seen everything, which was going to earn me another spanking at the very least. He would probably want to take me into the dunes to fuck me as well, in front of Stacey, and we were laughing at the prospect of what was about to happen as we walked back along the beach, hand in hand. I'd been in the sea to wash, and was now wet all over, Stacey too, our naked bodies glistening in the bright sunlight. As we approached Magnus he was grinning.

'That was quite a performance, girls, and in front of a couple of dozen French fishermen? Tut, tut.'

He was ready for me, his long, powerful legs extended to make a spanking lap, his beer thrust into the sand to leave his huge hands free to be used on my bottom. I looked down, folding my hands in my lap, a gesture at once pathetic and contrite, also sure to earn me a longer, harder spanking, as would a little teasing encouragement.

'Are you going to spank me, sir?'

'Yes, Lucy, I'm going to spank you, but, in all fairness, don't you think you ought to be spanked too, Stacey?'

I looked around in surprise, expecting a sharp answer, but it never came. She was biting her lip and looked more than a little embarrassed. The grin on Magnus's face was close to demonic.

'Stacey was very kind after you'd left, and allowed me to spank her, purely for my pleasure and not at all hard, but still.'

I turned to Stacey, who hung her head in deep embarrassment and spoke in a whisper.

'I ... I got a hot bottom. It was quite nice, really, and now ...'

'She lets me spank her before sex, occasionally, but I've always said it should be for when she's naughty, and she's been coming around to the idea. I suspect that peeing all over another girl and then sitting on her face counts as naughty, don't you? Well, Stacey, do you feel you ought to be spanked?'

She didn't answer immediately but just stood there, making little patterns in the sand with her toes, and when she did speak it was in a barely audible whisper.

'Oh, all right, you can spank me.'

Magnus gave a contented chuckle, then turned to me.

'Allowing yourself to be peed on also counts as naughty, Lucy, not to mention masturbating while it's done, and with an audience. Come on, you're first.'

141

He was beckoning to me and I nodded, but even as I got across his knee I wasn't thinking so much of what was about to happen to me as of what would happen to Stacey once I'd been dealt with. She was going to be spanked, my beautiful, commanding friend, who did me so well and always, always stayed firm and in control. She was going to be bent over a man's knee to have her bottom slapped just like any other girl.

I got it quick and hard, my bottom given a firm, efficient roasting that left me clutching my cheeks and jumping up and down on my toes, as well as drawing cheers and clapping from the distant fishing boats. Stacey watched as before, except that instead of looking cool and superior she was pink-faced and fidgeting. I knew how she felt, from my own early experiences: knowing what a smacked bottom would do for her but having trouble accepting what that involved, submission to a man.

But she didn't make a fuss as she was put, bare and beautiful, into the classic spanking position, over a man's knee, a situation at once impossibly shameful and far too undignified for any woman to adopt, and yet in another way perfectly appropriate and just plain right. Her eyes were closed, her face working with shame, but she obviously wanted it done, and done in front of me. Magnus wanted to do it too, his expression stern but very, very satisfied as he laid one massive hand across her rear cheeks.

'Here we go, Stacey, this will be what, the third time? No, the fourth, but this is your first proper punishment, isn't it?'

I thought she'd take it like a big girl, and I'm sure she could have done, physically, but she was being punished and she knew it, which was just too much. She stayed down, her fingers and toes dug into the sand, quite still and very different to my own pathetic kicking and wriggling, but as her bottom began to bounce to the slaps her mouth opened wide and tears began to trickle from her eyes and roll slowly down her cheeks to splash on the dry sand beneath her face.

She looked beautiful, even dignified in a way, or at least far more dignified than I would have been in the same position, and there was no doubting her physical reaction. Her pussy soon started to cream, her sex lips puffy with excitement despite our roll in the cool sea, and as the spanking continued she began to gasp and push her bottom up, plainly ready for sex. Magnus stayed cool, spanking with firm, methodical smacks placed evenly across her bottom to turn both full cheeks a rich, glowing pink.

I knew his cock would be hard, as it had already been growing while I was over his lap and he always gets stiff from spanking a girl. He'd be ready, I was sure of it, but to my surprise he held back, waiting until Stacey finally broke, babbling apologies for her filthy behaviour and begging to be spanked harder and then fucked. She got both, her bottom treated to a last furious salvo of smacks before she was put on her knees and entered roughly from behind. Meanwhile I slid in beneath to lick her cunt and kiss his balls while they fucked, and at the last moment to take him deep in my mouth and drink down her cream and his spunk together.

Chapter Ten

It had been a wonderful weekend, but as I rode the TGV north on the Sunday evening I couldn't stop brooding. When I'd accepted the job in Paris I'd known it would come at a cost to my relationships with Magnus and Stacey. That's all part of having a career, but I hadn't expected them to find solace together quite so quickly, or so much. It had always been the two of them enjoying me, with very little interaction between them, but that was no longer true. When we were together everything had been lovely; now I was on my own. Then there was the situation at work, and with Adrienne, which had been thrown into stark relief by the perfect balance of tenderness and cruelty with which Magnus and Stacey had treated me.

The most important thing was to discover whether Adrienne had intended to stop me going away for the weekend. That meant another heavy conversation, something I could have done without, but I had to know, especially before accepting any punishment she might have in mind for me to make up for my absence. I thought she'd be waiting for me in my apartment, quite possibly with Marcelon and a few friends to put me through my paces before she took me to bed. But she wasn't there, which came as a relief as I was still sore from the poundings I'd had over the weekend, although Magnus and Stacey had put me on the train with a hot bottom and I didn't mind playing as long as it wasn't too rough.

I decided to go and see her, and as I climbed the stairs I was thinking of what I ought to say. I approached her door, hoping she was in and on her own, but paused as I heard voices coming from her apartment. They were too faint to make out, but by turning my key ever so carefully and easing the door open an inch I was able to hear without giving myself away. I'd expected Marcelon, perhaps other men, but the first voice to speak was less deep but richer, a voice that held the promise of sex: Sabrina.

'… shouldn't worry. She's a sweetie.'

Adrienne answered, her voice urgent, almost pleading. 'But that's the trouble! She needs a mistress, or a master for that matter, but somebody to control her, somebody she knows will always be in charge.'

I froze, fairly sure who "she" was – myself – although I couldn't understand why Adrienne sounded so upset.

'Maybe she's more flexible than you think?' Sabrina continued.

Adrienne answered with a sigh. 'No. It's the classic pattern, you see. Because she has to make all the decisions at work, she needs to give in to somebody else in a relationship. If she finds out the truth she'll drop me, probably for Marcelon. I couldn't bear that!'

Her words and the tone of her voice suggested her feelings for me were much stronger than I'd imagined. I'd never realised she felt so insecure, and I wanted to reassure her because, whatever happened, I wouldn't be taking up with Marcelon. He was big and rough, a real turn-on when it came to sex, and a wonderful spanker, but he'd be far too demanding as a lover, expecting me to cook and clean and generally play the obedient little woman. I may like to be abused, but I'm nobody's skivvy.

Adrienne continued, and now her voice sounded husky and thick with need.

'And when I did it to her! You can imagine how I felt, wishing it was me, so badly, or both of us together, with you to do what's necessary.'

She finished with a moan so deep and needy it sounded as if she was playing with herself as she talked. Obviously she had a secret, something she was embarrassed about that she thought would make me leave her, but I couldn't imagine what it could be. Sabrina spoke again, her voice gentle and soothing.

'Now that would be nice, but don't worry, darling. I can look after you, and when the time comes –'

'No. I'd lose her, Sabrina.'

'No, you won't, darling. She's crazy about you, and you're ever so good.'

'Not good enough. Not for her. She's got girlfriends in London. She's been doing it for years!'

'I'm sure you're fine. She's ever so obedient to you.'

'Yes, but ... I don't know, I hope you're right, Sabrina, but I'm scared I'll lose her every time I send her to somebody else, and if I don't she'll get bored. She just takes it all for granted. She didn't even text me to say thank you for arranging for old man Montesquieu to spank her, or for the kidnap!'

It was true, if not for the reasons she imagined, and I was feeling guilty as Sabrina responded.

'The ungrateful little bitch! Never mind, punish her well and she'll learn. That's the way with a brat, just the way I trained you. Remember how I used to give you the strap if you didn't say thank you nicely?'

My mouth fell open in shock at the revelation, quickly confirmed by Adrienne's answer.

'Yes, and it was just what I needed. So was tonight. Thank you. I wish I could go to bed like this, but she'll be back soon and she'll need a whipping. Just think, if I could cuddle up in bed with her like this. You could have us both together.'

'Don't tease, darling.'

I heard a chair shift and the sound of kisses as Sabrina

prepared to leave. They'd been playing, which gave me a sudden pang of jealousy despite everything I'd been up to myself. More importantly, whatever they'd been up to, Adrienne had been on the receiving end. That was how it sounded, anyway, and maybe I should just have walked in on them, but what they'd said had put my head in a whirl. I needed to think and if I didn't move fast I'd be caught – Sabrina would see me or hear me if I tried to go back down the stairs.

Fortunately the landing window was wide open to the hot summer night. I closed the apartment door and straightaway hauled myself out onto the leads, where I lay silent and still as Adrienne said goodnight to Sabrina. She giggled as they kissed again and Sabrina called her a naughty girl, leaving me more puzzled than ever. I had to know what she was up to, preferably without giving myself away, and the moment the door had closed again I moved carefully across to the window of her apartment and peered in.

Adrienne stood in the kitchen, pouring herself a drink from a bottle of pastis, her feet bare, her petite body naked beneath a see-through peignoir. It wasn't the black one she normally wore, but pink and trimmed with a broad, lacy froufrou that hid her curves – but not the fact that, rather than the frilly panties I'd have expected, her middle was wrapped in a big puffy nappy.

* * *

I should have been whipped that night, but when Adrienne came over to my apartment I was sitting waiting for her in the chair she would have chosen had she arrived first. She'd taken her time to change, as I knew she would, and she stepped through the door in what I can only describe as a bitch suit. Her heels were high and black and shiny, her slender legs clad in stockings that rose to disappear under the hem of a knee-length skirt that clung to the contours of her hips and was so tight she could only walk with tiny, precise steps. She was in a corset, black and laced tight to push her small high breasts up and out, with her nipples sticking up through the lace where she'd let her smart black jacket fall open. Black gloves extended above each elbow, a black velvet choker circled her neck and her hair was coiled up under a neat veiled hat. In one hand she held her dog whip, ready for my bottom.

She looked so good, so strong and dominant, that I nearly gave in. My deepest instincts were telling me to strip naked, get down on all fours, crawl to her, beg to be beaten and reduced to a sweaty, blubbering mess before she stuck the whip handle up my cunt and put her bottom in my face. It took all my willpower not to do it. I stayed as I was, sitting back in the chair with my legs crossed, watching her as she watched me. She spoke first.

'Well, Cochonette, don't you think you ought to be on your knees? Why are you even dressed? Why are you dressed like that?'

Her last question showed just the faintest hint of uncertainty, and with good reason. I'd known she'd take her time to get dressed up for me, and I hadn't wasted it. I didn't have her impressive wardrobe to choose from, but skintight black jeans, boots, a black T-shirt and my three-quarter-length leather coat gave a similar effect, enhanced by my height as I stood up, towering over her by a good six inches.

'I'm not on my knees, Adrienne, because tonight it's your turn to be on your knees, and, more importantly, over mine.'

'What? How dare you? You need a sharp lesson in who's boss, Lucy Salisbury. Now get on the floor, you little fuck pig, and maybe, just maybe, I'll stick to fifty cuts for your insolence!'

I shook my head and folded my arms across my chest, looking down at her. Her face was twisted in fury, and if I hadn't heard her talking to Sabrina I'd never have suspected for an instant that she wasn't everything she seemed, an arrogant, cuntsure dominatrix about to put some silly little bitch in her proper place. But I'd heard, and I'd seen, and I held my poise even as she stepped in close and spoke in a cold, threatening hiss.

'On the floor, Lucy, right now.'

'I don't think so, Adrienne.'

She reached out left-handed, meaning to grab my wrist and twist me around so that my arm would be behind

151

my back and my bottom pushed out, allowing her to go to work on me as she pleased. And it would have been great to be held with my arm twisted behind my back as I was hauled out of my jeans and panties to leave me bare, then to be whipped as I squealed and begged and wriggled in her grip. Unfortunately she had a lesson to learn.

I twisted my hand to grip her wrist and held her tightly as I let myself fall back into the chair. She came with me, caught off balance, her tiny body pulled down by my weight and strength, straight over my knee and into spanking position. As she found herself bottom up across my legs she cried out in wordless outrage and tried to jerk back, but she was simply too weak. An instant later I'd got her in an arm lock, helpless for all her desperate wriggling and her frantic and far from ladylike kicking. Her outrage gave way to panic as she found her voice.

'What are you doing, Lucy? You can't! You can't ... you ...'

She couldn't say it, and I found myself laughing, then stopped abruptly as I caught the edge of hysteria in my own voice.

'*Spank*, Adrienne, that's the word you want, spank, spank, spank, what naughty girls have done to their bottoms, and what I am about to do to yours.'

This time she just screamed, a sound so full of despair I'd have let go if it hadn't been for what I'd heard – and if I hadn't recognised a reflection of how I would react if put in the same sorry situation. She couldn't stop this happening, not just because I was so much stronger than her but because deep down it was exactly what she wanted. But still she fought me, her lithe little body squirming in my grip and her legs kicking up and down with frantic energy. If I wanted to do this, I was going to have to conquer her – and I did, holding her firmly in place as I unzipped the tight black skirt and tugged it down over her hips to get her bare. As her rounded little bottom came on show I played my trump card.

'There we are, Adrienne, over the knee and bare bottom, just the way a naughty little girl like you ought to be when she has to be spanked. And you are going to be spanked, make no mistake about it – and do you know what I'm going to do after I've spanked you?'

She could have told me to fuck off, and her breathing was still hard and angry, but all she did was shake her head, which I took as the first sign of submission.

'What I am going to do, Adrienne, is put you in a nappy. How will that feel?'

I thought she'd start fighting again, one last desperate effort to save her dignity in the sure knowledge that she was going in her nappy whether she liked it or not, but she reacted with a low whimper, broken by a word, and went limp across my knee, sobbing her heart out as she pushed up her bottom for my attention. My mouth curved into a smile as I settled my hand across her round little cheeks, and with that I began to spank, talking to her as her bottom began to bounce and quiver to the slaps.

'No panties, I see. I suppose that was to make it easier for you to get your bottom in my face once I'd been whipped, but it's certainly going to make it easier for me to get you into your nappy, darling. Now isn't that ironic?'

She wasn't taking it too well, although maybe no worse than I would have in her position. She was still wriggling a lot and kicking about, squealing too, but now purely in pained reaction to the stinging slaps I was planting on her already pink cheeks, rather than from any desire to resist. In fact she'd given in completely; the word 'nappy' had obviously got to her. But if that was her thing, then spanking is mine, and I had no intention of denying myself.

I did her well, smacking the sweet little bum I'd kissed and licked so often, until she was rosy all over, her hips pushed up for more and her cheeks spread to show off the tight dark spot of her anus and her cunt lips. She was soaking, as turned on by her punishment as I'd ever been, for all her sobs and snivels, but again, I'd have been the same. I could have made her come so easily, made her beg to be spanked harder still as I rubbed her off, but that would have left the job half done.

When I finally stopped she made no effort to get up, for all that she knew what was coming. I had everything ready that I needed, tucked out of sight behind my chair in a bag, which I pulled out as I began to talk to her once more.

'There we are, all warm and rosy, and I'm sure you feel a lot better for your spanking, don't you? You see, it's nice really, because it's what every naughty girl needs, regularly, and you are no exception, Adrienne, any more than I am. Now, a little powder for your pussy, if you could open up a little more, please?'

As I spoke I began to shake the powder between her thighs, which she'd opened on command, showing off her cunt without the slightest attempt at concealment. I used plenty of powder and patted it well in to leave her dry and fresh, but for the moist pink slit between her lips and the hole of her vagina. She was so turned on she was actually open, and I slid a finger in just for fun, making her moan before I turned my attention to her bottom.

'Now your cheeks, and in between … and just a little dab of cream for your bottom hole.'

I spread her cheeks as I spoke, holding her anus wide as I shook more powder over it, then taking a tube of baby lotion and squeezing a little out into the hole. She began to sob again, but broke off with a little cry as I eased one finger into her bottom to make sure she was nice and creamy all the way up. I'd had it done to me often enough, and I could imagine how she felt with her smacked bottom being fingered. I chuckled in sheer devilment.

'There we are, all fresh and clean and creamy. Now for your nappy, a nice big towelling nappy, just like the one Sabrina put you in just now. Oh, yes, Adrienne, I was listening, and I saw you through the window. That's how I know your little secret, and that's why you're going in nappies.'

She finally found her voice.

'You … you …'

I knew what she wanted to say.

'Bitch? Now come on, that's not fair, is it? This is what you want, you said so yourself, and if you got spanked too, well, you have to allow me my little quirks.'

'No, Lucy, I –'

'Hush, Adrienne, it's too late to back out now. Now lift your tummy.'

It was, and she went quiet as she raised her body to let me slip the big white towel under her tummy. Her legs were still wide open, and I made quick work of putting her into the nappy, turning it up over her bottom and tying off the sides, just as she had once done for me. The result was good but not perfect, because she still looked like the perfect little bitch queen, except that she'd been put in a nappy. I stood her up to inspect her and her thumb went straight into her mouth, her eyes wide and moist as she looked at me, awaiting instructions.

'Strip, naked for now, although I might let you put

a top on later, if you're lucky. And you're to put your hair up in bunches.'

She obeyed without question, peeling off her beautiful dominant clothes to leave herself stark naked but for the puffy white nappy around her middle. I lifted my top and one side of my bra to cup my breast for her, at which her eyes showed a final brief flicker of defiance. Then she curled herself into my lap and suckled at the teat as I stroked her hair. She began to masturbate as she sucked, the final act of surrender, but as I slipped a hand down the front of her nappy to take over I was wondering if she'd ever be able to deal with my own needs again.

* * *

I needn't have worried. Once she'd come down from her submissive high she was her old self again and took her revenge on me the moment I came home on Monday evening after work. No sooner was I through the door of my apartment than she'd frogmarched me into the bedroom, where I was made to strip and put on the bed in a kneeling position with my upturned bottom stuck out towards the window. The curtains were open a crack, and she told me the Commandant was watching through binoculars. Then she stuck courgettes up my pussy and bumhole and gave me a whipping that left me sweaty and gasping on the bed. I had my face sat

157

on and afterwards I was made to cook ratatouille in the nude for her and the Commandant, before going down on him as he sipped an after-dinner cognac.

Once he'd gone home we talked, as equals, smoothing out all the little bumps in our relationship and agreeing on what was and was not acceptable. I had to put a lot of effort into reassuring her that I wasn't going to run off as soon as I met somebody more experienced, but when we went to bed that night we made love in a way we'd never done before, cuddled together to kiss and lick and stroke each other's bodies until we'd both reached orgasm, although we also both had very warm bottoms.

Now that my relationship with Adrienne was as I wanted it, only one problem remained: M. Montesquieu. With his avuncular manner and habit of drinking at least one bottle of wine with lunch, it could only be a matter of time before he accidentally gave the game away. I could read the lustful twinkle in his eyes every time he spoke to me, I could feel his gaze lingering on my rear view as I walked about the office, and he'd become far more open and friendly than was normal in a professional relationship of our kind.

To make matters worse, I badly wanted to be spanked by him. He was exactly the right sort of man to do it, big and paternal but quite capable of being dirty with me once my panties were down and my bottom nicely warm. I could get it any time I wanted it, by waiting until everybody else had gone home then taking a trip across his knee for a bit of old-fashioned discipline before sucking his cock and going home to Adrienne with a hot bottom and a bellyful of spunk. It was lovely, too lovely, because eventually we were going to get caught.

I could picture it all too easily, the utter disgrace of dismissal and the appalled reaction of my senior colleagues to the discovery that I got spanked by my boss. The story was sure to get out, and would be round the industry in days. I'd get sacked for breach of the appropriate conduct clause in my contract and even if I did manage to get another job life would be unbearable. Everyone I worked with would be picturing how I'd look turned across a man's knee with my panties pulled down and my bottom pink from spanking. Worse still, the scenario was just the sort of thing I like to get off on, so for all my very real concerns it was impossible to think about it without wanting to masturbate.

He dealt with me three times during the week and then invited me around on the Sunday with the clear implication that I could expect some more. I asked if I could bring Adrienne, unable to resist the temptation of getting her over his knee too, but determined to have a serious talk with him about work once the fun bit was over. He agreed, but to my surprise we weren't alone. We arrived to find Nana in the kitchen, naked but for a pinafore, with her bare black bottom quivering slightly as she worked at grating carrots. I'd thought M. Montesquieu seemed a little shifty when he let us in, but he was now grinning as he clapped his hands together.

'Yes, as you see, I am not alone, and indeed I have an announcement to make. Your arrival in Paris has breathed new life into me, Lucy, and into the company. I am no longer needed, and you have taught me that I was wrong to assume that I am beyond the age at which I can enjoy female company. That is why I have decided to retire, with a strong recommendation to head office that you take over my position, while Nana has kindly agreed to join me at my place in Provence, haven't you, my dear?'

Nana had come out of the kitchen, smiling broadly. I responded in kind. I wasn't sure exactly what was going on, or how their arrangement would turn out, but my problem had been solved at a stroke. We'd even be able to visit them in the south of France. Meanwhile I could no doubt train Commandant Arnauld to spank me properly, but that was all in the future. For the moment, celebrations were clearly in order. A bottle of champagne was chilling in a bucket, but it could wait until M. Montesquieu had got my panties down, and Adrienne's too, for one more punishment in Paris.

www.ingramcontent.com/pod-product-compliance
Ingram Content Group UK Ltd.
Pitfield, Milton Keynes, MK11 3LW, UK
UKHW022259180325
456436UK00003B/153